I0623936

By: Cheraee C.

THE SHADIEST MISSION EVER

MOCY PUBLISHING
WWW.MOCYPUBLISHING.COM

Detroit, Michigan

The Shadiest Mission Ever

ISBN 978-1-940831-12-1
Copyright © 2015 by Cheraee C.

Published by Mocy Publishing, LLC.
Website: www.mocypublishing.com
Email: info@mocypublishing.com

Honorable Mentions

Casino Bailey

Sandra B.

Terance Drake

MUA Rochelle Darlene

Table of Contents

Please be advised this book contains heavy, urban literary language using slang, Ebonics, profanity, and street terms. It also contains very strong, articulate verbs, adverbs, adjectives, and so forth. This literary language is a part of a genre Cheraee C. created called intellectual, hood fiction.

Chapter 1: Shady Intent

Clinging onto her hospital gown like a souvenir, Omani refused to take the thin, cotton eyesore off.

"Omani please take that infirmary rag off. I can't be wandering around in public with you looking like a mental case."

"I don't want too; this gown is the closest emblem of motherhood I have left to Amory besides my cervical stitches so I'm not taking it off until we get her back," Omani proceeded to fold her arms together like a spoiled rich kid who's credit card got declined.

"I promise you were going to get her back, but you got to lose the grandma suit. You look like an outcast right now. Nobody is going to take us criminally serious if we both aren't dressed to par."

Ready to transition from grieving mother to stone cold killer, Omani finally decided to ease out her hospital threads. It had been weeks since Omani wore real clothes.

Since Omani and Onyx were on a mission, Onyx stepped out and chose some swanky pieces for his baby mother from her favorite boutique. Her spirits were lower than an old juke box trying to play a blues song. Her gloomy days were just temporary though because her and Onyx were about to impose their stratagem of retribution.

"I never wanted you to see my dark side Omani, but now the shit is inevitable."

"What are you talking about Onyx? Have you ever even owned a gun, loaded a gun. Or shot a gun before? I think not."

"You got jokes Omani. Let me tell you a little bit about my thuggish ruggish ways."

REWIND: Once upon a time, Onyx was an assembly line worker for the big 3 at the Ford Rouge Factory. He used to break niggas in the crannies of a warehouse for the owner of an automotive cartel whose name was Fess. Factory plants were colossal and earsplitting, and unless somebody pulled a fire alarm or spoke into an intercom, you wouldn't be able to hear a man cry for help even if he howled like a wolf.

Fess had economical ties with the big 3 and ties to the big 3's workers. Fess had at least a 1000 ways of getting money and two of those ways included pushing cocaine through the Ford plants and using company vehicles to push weight and company drivers. He proved that it was definitely some slick jokers in this world, and even though there was lots of money to be made and getting made in this organization, a thief was always being birthed every 60 seconds. After Fess saw Onyx put his paws on this worker Mitch, he knew off rip he wanted Onyx to be his hitta. Three perfect jabs and Onyx ended up putting Mitch in a coma. Mitch shouldn't have been lying on his baby dick and telling all the other workers at the plant he smashed Omani. At that time, nobody was smashing Omani except for Onyx. Onyx warned Mitch the first time he heard Mitch talking cash shit about how he was going to fuck Omani, how he knew Omani was digging him. Mitch didn't take heed to Onyx's forewarning though. Purposely, Mitch kept insulting and disrespecting Omani with his irritating and irrational ass insinuations. All Onyx wanted to do was his job, but Mitch made him snap like a camera. If he got fired, he got fired, so fucking be it. Onyx tried to ignore Mitch, but his ignorance was too flamboyant for that. Anybody who puts a co-worker in a coma should've been sued, fired, or facing criminal charges, but not Onyx. Fess was too impressed by Onyx's heavyweight skills that he had to promote Onyx to his team.

"So Onyx you know why your in my office right? Fess cross-examined his new protégé.

"Y'all honestly can just fire me over the phone. I don't need no sit-down to get fired." Onyx stood up as if he said his peace ready to dip.

"I would never fire somebody with such lethal hands when I can utilize their services."

"What's the catch?"

"Long story short, I'm a business man and niggas love to get out of line with me. When they get out of line you ruff them up however you want too. I'll pay you five bands a thrashing. If you refuse my offer then you can consider yourself fired and remove your rambunctious ass from my premises."

Precisely, Onyx envisioned all the bands he could make just to KO a bunch of hand-picked, weak niggas every other blue moon and he was down for the challenge. It wasn't like he really had an affirmative choice anyways.

"I'm down," and just like that any nigga that fucked over Fess got served a knuckle sandwich by Onyx. Fucking with Onyx and his fists you either ended up in a coma, in ICU, or in a morgue. Everything was cool until Fess disappeared off the face of Detroit. With Onyx's reputation in mind he took this opportunity as a way to put his Ford days behind him and resign.

$

Little did Omani know that Amory was not Onyx's only child. Two years ago, when Omani and Onyx were on expendable terms, he fathered a daughter named Corrine by a woman named Cortina. His daughter Corrine had the exact, same birthday as his new daughter Amory. When Onyx was at the hospital with Omani, it took him everything in his power not to have an emotional breakdown over Corrine or new fatherhood.

When Corrine was born, Onyx was locked up in the pen upstate. Somehow Cortina got into some trouble with Child Protective Services and their daughter was put into foster care. Onyx called and called Cortina to find out exactly what the bitch had done, but Cortina never answered Onyx's calls. Whether Cortina had somebody else in the picture or not was none of Onyx's concern. He just wanted to make sure his baby girl was straight.

Since Onyx was incarnated he couldn't save Corrine from the evil system so the state took it upon itself to terminate the rights of both parents all due to the severity of offenses against Cortina's and Onyx's inability to be active parents.

The only person besides the parents who knew about this secret child was Onyx's mother Oni, but since Onyx didn't have an ongoing son-mother type of bond with her his secret wasn't exposable. Onyx begged his mother Oni to take care of her granddaughter until he came home, but she refused. What type of grandmother would refuse to care for her only grandchild? Oni didn't have any reason to refuse caring for baby Corrine temporarily. No matter what pretenses stood against Corrine, Oni blatantly refused. She claimed she wanted nothing to do with Onyx, his life, or anybody in it. This situation is the reason why Onyx and

Oni don't have and will never have a functional relationship. As far as he was concerned, he didn't have a mother, he raised himself.

When Onyx got released from jail from doing a bid on a probation violation, he tried to find Corrine, but she was lost in the system. It was like she had a new identity all of a suddenly. Besides, Onyx didn't have any legal rights to Corrine anymore so in court he didn't stand a chance. He didn't want too, but he had to let the memory of Corrine go. Hopefully, one day they would be reunited someway, somehow.

Now that he had baby Amory that was his second chance of true fatherhood. He was hoping this time nothing would go wrong, but it was too late for that because everything that could possibly be wrong was wrong. It was like Onyx wasn't meant to be a father because every baby he has had has experienced some type of adversity because they can't even reach the age of 1 without walking a thin line. Onyx better hope and pray that Omani never finds out about his other child, because if she does Onyx is probably going to be buried up under a viaduct somewhere. It didn't matter that this was a child that Onyx fathered while the two was on a break, it was the fact that Onyx felt comfortable and attached enough to let his sperm swim in another bitches' ovaries while the two was on a break is exactly how Omani was going to see it. It will be no coming back for Onyx so hopefully nobody ever leaks his secret.

$

PLAY: Now here Onyx was still riding with his black-hearted girl Omani about to take lives and kill things. They were two thoroughbred parents willing to abominate a whole planet for their precious pride and joy-Amory. Out of nowhere a sense of pleasure came over Onyx like a typical man. He began fondling her breasts, her nipples, and her areolas with his hands in a very teasing way. Then he lifted up her shirt and pulled her perky breasts out her bra one at a time trading attention from one to the other. Usually, Omani was never aroused by breast fondling and titty sucking, but today was different. As inconsolable as Omani was she couldn't help, but to throw her head back, arch her back, bite her lips a bit, moan, and tremble. Then Onyx took his fingers and began circling and twirling them on the outer origins of her vagina. Both of them were ready to knock each other off physically, but mentally Omani couldn't take it there so Omani pushed Onyx flat back into his seat.

"Chill Onyx I can't do this."

"Why not you know you want too?"

"Doesn't matter I just had a baby and our baby just got kidnapped. This isn't the time or the place for this."

"I think we should have sex before we go killing folks. Who knows this could be our last chance to have sex with each other. It's no telling what or where the road ahead is going to lead us to or through."

"In your mind you better scroll down memory lane of all the times we fucked because that's the best that I can do for you right now," and just like that the rapture was lost. It was time for them to settle some scores and for them to be the leaders of their amber alert. Amory Mitchell was coming home, Lindsay Chambers was going to die slowly, and both Onyx and Omani were going to see to it.

Chapter 2: The Pit of Insecurity

These days Paradise would never emotionally be in the land of milk and honey. Paradise currently resided in Cahill's main house in Michigan while he flew back and forth to St. Louis, Missouri being a mayor in the public eye and a shady diabolist off the clock.

Cahill was too scatterbrained to maintain a healthy relationship with his puerile little thrill. All the private investigators, lie detector tests, or spy cams in the world wouldn't be enough to suppress his paranoia. Cahill had 24-hour surveillance on Paradise and not even 1% of it could connect her to disloyalty. No matter what innocence she claimed or modeled, all women were bonafide cheaters and that was their main prerogative in life; to cheat. Cheat on a good man with long money. Despite, a lack of evidence, he was predetermined Paradise was creeping with her watchman Rock. It's a shame that Cahill had all that political power and no trust, but I guess its politics that say to trust your instincts. It was more tabloids prowling around the streets about dirtbag politicians then unfaithful women, so if anybody should have a watchful eye it should be Paradise.

What was the genius point of hiring a security guard let alone a male security guard if all Cahill was just gonna blame Paradise of cheating? If Cahill hired a female security guard, Paradise wondered if the cheating claims would still exist. Since Cahill was the king of insecurity, the cheating allegations would still be vigorous no matter what the gender type was or sexual orientation. According to Cahill, his eyes don't lie, and he was drained from all the signs he had in his mind.

Paradise never received proper or any sweet greetings and salutations from Cahill. Whenever he walked through or left the corridors it was nothing, but drama and insecurity.

"Why the fuck you lounging around here in a robe?" Cahill badgered Paradise after he grappled open her robe like he was about to take it there and saw that her body was completely bare. Instead of getting an erection and engulfing in some intimate, love-making, Cahill chose to fuss, convict, and argue.

"I just got out the shower Cahill. You can go check the tub. My shower cap is still wet and the bathroom mirror still has condensation on it. Please don't come home with this cheating bullshit again," Paradise pulled her robe back closed.

"Or what? What you goin do? You goin run off and be with Rock because you can leave and go be with that nigga right now. Y'all not goin keep playing me in my own got damn house!"

"If anybody is getting played it's me; a guilty accuser symbolizes a guilty conscience. I know exactly how you politicians get down, and I know how you use your money to lure women into your wicked world. That's why I never been your girl in the spotlight and you keep me locked up in these walls like an inmate so nobody will know that your in a official relationship."

"I like to keep my relationships private and you know this so don't try to flip the script. You can go out there and be a little street rat if you want too, I bet you want find your way back here. Once Lindsay finds a way to leech onto your ass, your just going to be another dead body. Did you forget? You can't go outside and play like everybody else because your a little bandit that likes to steal and a lethargic criminal who didn't finish the job. Your a runaway and I'm housing you and loving you despite your flaws."

"I could've stayed where I was at for this shit. I don't know why I let myself come to Michigan with you."

Lucky for Paradise, Cahill didn't hear the last of her sarcastic comments because if he did, Paradise probably wouldn't even have a mouthpiece to even speak out of. Like every relationship when things were good they were good, and when things were bad they were all bad.

Sexually, nothing I mean nothing had ever popped off between Paradise and Rock, but a week ago they shared a passionate kiss right smack, dab, and center on each other's lips. Before the kiss even happened Cahill was throwing his cheating accusations all around. Guess he became a fortune teller overnight and could predict the future. He must've felt as if Paradise didn't cheat on him yet she was going too eventually. Let's not forget about the lack of sex; you can't be living in a house with a man with a working penis and not having any sex. Somebody was going to break and since Cahill knew what he did behind closed doors, he knew Paradise was going to be up to something too. Cahill was ready to get rid of her; he just wasn't team Paradise anymore, and he really sensed that she had a thing for Rock and Rock had a thing for her.

However, he wasn't going to let either one of them betray him even though technically it was fair game.

A week ago Rock played his cards right on cue. Once Rock was positive that Cahill had officially left the building, he went to go sweet-talk Paradise out her panties or at least stimulate the panty-dropping process. Rock wasn't supposed to bother Paradise unless she requested his services, but today was different. Rock overheard Paradise and Cahill arguing tough before Cahill went to work so he felt like being bold. Rock always hearkened to the two of them arguing. Clearly, his game revolved around vulnerability so Rock planted a few light knocks on the boss's bedroom door.

"Who's knocking and why?"

"It's me Rock; I'm just checking on you. I'm usually being your butler by now."

"Go away Rock!"

"Come on now Paradise; I'm the last person you should shut out. Just watch I'll be right back."

Paradise wasn't doing anything out of the ordinary, but lying in the bed pouting, waving her feet in the air with her head sunk into her folded arms. She wondered what Rock was up to. Rock went to the kitchen to make Paradise her favorites; some sweet iced tea, and a grilled turkey sandwich on Texas Toast. Paradise heard loud noises coming from the kitchen and smelled some rich, tasty aromas soaring through the air so she decided to come out of her cave. Soon as she hit the kitchen, Rock had everything finish on a platter he was about to serve her.

"You did this for me?"

"Yeah, I don't know why, but I did."

Paradise started digging into her homemade afternoon delight.

"You got something on your lips, let me get that for you," Rock insisted. After he wiped the bread crumbs off of her lips he decided to kiss her.

"I've been waiting on you to do that for a long time. I'm feeling you too and just so you know me and Cahill were arguing about you. He's been accusing me of cheating with you from sun up to sundown."

"I see and hear everything that's why you should let him go and come be with me."

"He's never goin let us be together; we will both be dead before we make it out of Michigan."

"You let me worry about Cahill; I know exactly how to deal with him. The beauty of the past and knowledge is a powerful thing, but first I need to know if you really ready to leave him or not because I'm done working for that foul, knavish piece of shit. I've done work for senators, mayors, governors, presidential candidates, etc the list goes on. Cahill is aware of that yet he hires me to be his girlfriend's house sitter? Nobody is going to get away with underestimating me. I only agreed to take his offer because I plan on sinking Cahill Caesar. I didn't plan on catching feelings for you in the process of all this, but I have so what are you gonna do?"

"I choose you now; when are we going to leave?"

"Just give me a little time I have something major in the works. I promise you I will get you out of this."

During the last past month, Paradise and Rock had been getting fairly acquainted. Each time Cahill and Paradise argued, or even if they didn't argue, Rock always made time to interface with Paradise whenever Cahill wasn't around as did Paradise. Paradise didn't hold back anything either so she didn't have a problem with informing him about the whole Passive and Lindsay fiasco. At that point, Rock didn't hold back that he knew Passive and they were cool. Paradise was ashamed of her errors and just knew that Rock was going to unlatch feelings for her after listening to how Paradise betrayed his friend, but she was wrong. Rock was very indulgent; it would be immature of him to be angry at her for her actions during a time when he didn't know her. He was going to take whatever measures he had to take to bring peace to everybody he loved, and hell to everybody he hated.

Chapter 3: Pass-out

The most idiosyncratic day ever was the day Cahill came home earlier than usual gripping a grocery bag in like he was about to cook up a feast.

"Cahill I got to make a run so I'll return thereafter."

"See you when you get back then," Cahill waved off Rock.

Rock hopped in his car and called his secret weapon.

"Hello," the secret weapon greeted.

"Seems I can meet with you sooner than we thought so where am I coming to?"

"Do you recall that Biggby Coffee we were talking about in Livonia?"

"I do so I'll see you there shortly."

Passive and Elvia were riding together as always like sisters of a gun. They were both ready to get the scoop on Cahill Caesar because Passive always had a ready clip for him.

Shortly, after Passive and Elvia grabbed a table Rorric also known as Rock joined them.

$

Rorric Hill was Cahill's current bodyguard, and the ex-bodyguard of Passive's father Syrian Boone. Rorric was always watching over the Boone family and had taken a bullet for Passive's father before and that earned him a special place in Passive's heart. Passive had a high level of trust and comfortableness with Rorric. A lot of people approached Passive at her father's funeral; everybody was pretending like they were so empathetic knowing damn well they only came to the funeral for the food. The day of the funeral is always hugs, kisses, flowers, and sympathy cards, and the day after everyone disappears into thin air like vapor and you never see them again. The only person that Passive kept in contact with was Rorric because he had an idle role in the Boone family; it wasn't anything counterfeit about him.

$

"So what's good Rorric?"

"What's been good with you Sive? I see you looking more beautiful than ever." Elvia thought Rock's nickname for Passive was cute and she speculated what Passive would say if she called her Sive.

"   "Your complements are always welcome, but let's get down to business."

"I know you've been waiting to get your bullets on Cahill and now is the time. I work for him again and I know everything you need to know, but I have something to request from you."

"What's that?"

"His girlfriend is your enemy so I ask that you drop your beef with her for this information because you have bigger fish to fry."

"My enemy who?"

"Paradise."

"The bitch that robbed me and helped kidnap me in Missouri? You expect me to let that shit ride?"

"All these years Cahill has been working under the table with Lindsay. I know this for a fact. I watch him like a Seahawk and one day he had me chauffeuring him around town. We ended up Downtown by the Riverwalk. He told me to sit still when he got out the car; he said he would be back shortly. I knew he had to be meeting someone up there because he ain't the make transactions in the street type so I followed behind him. He was sitting on the bleachers talking to a strange woman who he addressed as Lindsay. I figured this had to be your Lindsay because she was firmly speaking of you. Their whole conversation revolved around your name; Lindsay told Cahill he had 90 days to kill you basically or she was going to kill you for killing her mother. In his own little way he's still playing the godfather card, but we both know he killed your parents because nobody else wanted your parents dead on this planet. Plus I was there I saw him do it; he caught me off guard. I was there when he killed your mother, and I was there when he made the hit to have your father killed in jail." Passive couldn't believe her ears; all this time that her mother has been dead and nobody leaked a squeal. If Rorric was there how many more witnesses were out there withholding information? It wasn't like Rorric was Cahill's top guy or right hand man. Rorric was just another watchdog he trusted to be in his league.

"Why haven't you been confided in me about this? Why would you wait until now Rorric? I thought we was way better than that. I would never keep some shit like this away from you if I witnessed somebody kill somebody you love."

"Please don't make this personal Sive because it's not. Why do you think I stopped working for Cahill in the first place? It was because I know the real things that Cahill does behind closed doors. He doesn't deserve to be a mayor and he doesn't deserve to be alive. Why do you think I'm helping you? I chose to tell you now because back then you wasn't ready for this type of truth. You would've tried to kill Cahill on impulse and anybody can vouch that you never kill someone on impulse that's like committing suicide."

"So how did he kill her? That's the least you can do is tell me that."

"Come on now Passive you know I've said enough. I'm basically dry snitching right now because we share the same enemies. Knowing that Cahill is indeed the culprit that killed both of your parents is closure enough. I'm not feeding into any details because that's how people twist things around. After we put these two up under the dirt, I won't mind telling you what you want to know then. I think we should collaborate on writing a book and title it *The*

Evil Godfather. We can reveal all his dirty laundry in this book and I can let you know exactly how he killed your parents."

"So what's your game plan?"

"I'm gonna skip town with Paradise and simply give you my key and you can do whatever it is that you see fit to him. I know you are very shrewd when it comes to the politics of your malice so I know your going to fully dissect every aspect of Cahill before you just jump into the lion's den."

"I got back-up and we do everything according to a system. Just give me the rundown of his floor plan, weaponry, daily schedule, security system, visitors, neighbors, building overview, and any other specs you think of."

Rock dug in his pocket, pulled out a key, and slid it over to Passive.

"Here goes a copy of the key right here just to confirm my commitment to our pact."

"My binoculars are on just get me the info I asked for ASAP and give me the heads-up on the day you plan to skip town so I can work my magic."

"I'll be in touch Sive, and it was nice meeting your partner in crime, peace."

"Are you okay Passive, I know that was a lot to take in," Elvia asked very concerned about Passive's state of mind, but Passive never answered her. Passive was absolutely not expecting to hear the confirmations she heard during her meeting with Rock. She was gracious that she had longtime friends like Rock who always came in good handy when necessary. In all honesty, she couldn't blame Rock for not breaking his silence because who would want to be caught up in the wrath of a vengeful wife and daughter. Rock knew Passive had a merciless side and he didn't want to spark it, but what was done was done. It was no way Rock could let someone beat him to the punch, because Cahill was the kind to flip things on people and if he was given the opportunity he would flip the death of Passive's mother and father on Rock somehow, which would make Passive kill Rock. It was too late for that plan to work because Rock was one step of the shady, flaky Mayor Cahill. *I've been so self-consumed with Lindsay and getting payback on her for Smoke's family it's time I finally self-consume myself with my own family and avenging their deaths. They should've never been taken away from me; I can't believe how close proof really was to me, but Rock was right I wasn't ready then, but I am ready now.*

Parting ways, Passive didn't make it out of Biggby's Coffee without collapsing in front of Elvia. Elvia caught Passive in her arms before Passive could hit the ground.

"Shit!" Elvia cussed.

"We got to get her to a hospital now something is wrong. Nothing like this has ever happened before," Elvia told Rock.

"I believe you don't worry I'll carry her to y'all car and so it's not trouble I'll just follow you to the nearest hospital."

"Okay, but you don't have to stay. Once you put her in my car you can be headed on. I got it from here."

"Passive means a lot to me as she does to you. I'm not going to leave her side until I know she's okay."

In route to St. Mary Mercy Hospital, Elvia called Smoke to let him know that Passive had just fainted.

"What's going on Elvia?" Smoke answered.

"I'm on my way to St. Mary Mercy Hospital in Livonia. Passive just fainted and she's still unconscious so please meet me there."

"How did she faint? I'm sorry for asking that a person just faints. I'm on my way there."

Once Elvia reached the hospital, she parked her car in front of the Emergency Entrance, ran in and got a hospital employee to bring out a stretcher to put Passive on. Two nurses rushed out to her car with the stretcher, put Passive on it and wheeled her away. Elvia gave her keys to a valet driver so she could attend to her best friend/sister.

"Why the fuck are they just wheeling her away without letting somebody accompany her?" The doors to the ER were shut so there was nothing Elvia could do, but sit in the lobby until a nurse allowed her to go into the ER.

"Excuse me ma'am my sister is back there and nobody is with her," Elvia approached a woman holding a phone at the front desk.

"I can't let you back there; you have to wait until a doctor comes out and speaks to you."

"This is some bullshit!" Elvia yelled as Rock as he prompted her to have a seat.

"This is just hospital protocol, we can't do shit, but follow it."

As Elvia and Rock were seated by each other, in came Smoke who was already on tip because his wife was in a hospital and when he saw Elvia sitting by a strange male he got even more irate.

"Who the fuck is you homeboy?" Smoke hadn't seen Rock in years so he didn't recognize him or remember him from his father-in-law's funeral since that was Passive's friend.

"No need to be a tough tone I'm just here to make sure Sive is okay."

"Why the fuck you giving my wife pet names? Ain't nobody named Sive here!" Smoke charged after Rock sending blow after blow to his rib cage.

"Smoke, calm down get yourself together you acting berserk for no reason!" Elvia contained Smoke.

"Rock, please leave and let me and Smoke deal with this. I'll give you an update as soon as I get one."

The hospital worker heard the ruckus in the lobby and had to give her lobby guests her two cents.

"Y'all hoodlums can get up out here with all of that street shit coming up in here like y'all ain't got no got damn home training. This ain't no damn zoo y'all better take y'all asses to Royal Oak with the wild animals."

"Smoke, I've never seen you this upset before."

"And Passive has never been to the hospital before either since I've been with her so you have to understand how that is affecting me."

"Rock is a family friend of Passive's family. He used to guard her father Syrian. Does that ring a bell?" Smoke thought back, I mean way back, and felt like a complete ass.

"Oh, damn I remember that cat now."

"Oh well what's done is done."

Finally a doctor came out from the back asking for the family of Passive Mitchell and up jumped Smoke and Elvia.

"Hi, everyone I'm Doctor Blackwell," the doctor stated shaking the two pair of hands in front of him.

"I'm her husband Darnell and this is her sister Elvia."

"I'm sure Passive gave y'all a nice scare, but her and the baby are fine. Passive is two months pregnant and we had to give her a blood transfusion because she has severe anemia. Her iron level was too low and that's what caused her to faint. Sorry to say, but Passive falls up under the high-risk pregnancy category and will have to spend the duration of her pregnancy in the hospital. I hope you guys are ready to make this y'all new home."

"Isn't it some type of medicine she can take or something that can be done so she doesn't have to live in here for the next 7/8 months?"

"She's pregnant and there are just too many risks for her pregnancy not to be monitored. Passive could've lost the baby today if she would've come to the ER any later." Elvia and Smoke were still in shock off of the good news slash bad news.

"Can we see her then?"

"Please give her some time to rest. She needs as much rest as possible and to be in a low stress environment. Are you guys hearing me?"

"As you wish doc."

Chapter 4: Baby Mother Land

The shady chromosomes that were dominant in the Chamber hereditary were now replicating autosome actions in British's life. Every since Lindsay returned to the motor city it was like the dawn of a new era in British's self-centered, but insignificant, despicable life. Never had British been so counteractive until Lindsay infected her with her shady cancer.

Fact one was that Rue cheated on British and impregnated his mistress; fact two Rue let his mistress succeed in birthing their baby instead of forcing an abortion or making the bitch have a miscarriage. Fact three was that the mistress wasn't intimidated by British and continued to undermine her position in Rue's life. Fact four whether Tia had Rue's baby or not didn't mean he had to play daddy. British wanted Rue to be a deadbeat daddy at least request a paternity test before taking any or full responsibility of the child in question. There was a web of lies around whose

Tia's actual baby father was and since she lied about who the father was once, who says she wouldn't lie again.

Call it jealousy, but British was supposed to be the only woman to ever bear any of Rue's children, but yet she was still childless while his bedmate got to parade around town with that title and privilege. The fact that Rue was having unprotected sex with a shack job, and having unprotected sex with British was just mind-boggling. British thought that Rue was smarter than that: you never have raw sex with a chatelaine. There shouldn't have been any outside sex going on anyway especially when Rue could get any pleasure he wanted at home, but guess that pleasure was becoming too familiar to him. Sometimes a lurking man finds himself roaming and acting on his temptations and this was the case.

Instead of British leaving Rue for disrespecting her, all she wanted him to do was leave Tia alone and her baby, but their issues continued because he refused to abide by British's barter.

"Where in the fuck do you think you going?" British questioned Rue after she closed the fridge and felt him skulking past the kitchen.

"Why do you have to question me every time I go somewhere now?"

"You don't even say bye you just leave."

"The only way our communication is going to be back tight is if you stop associating my whereabouts to Tia. I'm sick of you trying to control the situation like you nutted up in her and got her pregnant."

"You still don't know if it is your nut that got her pregnant. You want to be a father that bad that you would claim a prostitute's baby?"

Rue flew from the hallway to the kitchen tired of dealing with British and her attitude. He sprung up on her, grabbed her chin, used his free hand to tickle her lips causing British to stick out her tongue, and him to grip her tongue ring so worthlessly British whole ambience shifted.

"I told you not goin stop me from seeing my son and you not goin disrespect the mother of my seed or keep questioning that being my seed. Clearly ain't nothing wrong with my sperm so check your pussy. I been trying to get you pregnant for years. You goin stop talking to me like you got a dick and I got a pussy. This might be your grandma's house, but while I'm in here I'm the man of this castle so chill out with your attitude because I'm the type of nigga who will rip your tongue out. Once a pool of British's tears began streaming from the bays of her eyes, Rue knew he had made his point and freed her tongue.

"I'm not fucking with her like that no more, I don't spend the night over there, and I always come home to you so re-evaluate your fucking place. Stop acting confused before your place permanently becomes somebody else's."

On that note, British presumed Rue was out to go see his son and was left to digest the jealous image of Rue with his son and Tia. Rue actually had other business to attend to in the streets, but it was hard for British to get the Tia fad out of her system. A man will tell you one thing and do another so regardless of what Rue said, British wasn't convinced.

Dying to see what tongue trauma Rue had done to her, British checked herself in the bathroom mirror. Silently hysterical British was infuriated by Rue's intent to hurt her. Her tongue appeared to be ripping and splitting so British removed her tongue piercing hoping that eventually it would heal. Bumps and swelling on the surface, British was shocked and couldn't believe that she was enduring her current pain over a side bitch. She was not about to let no little sally walker ass bitch get the best of her.

She was utterly disgusted with Rue and was beginning to lose all respect for him. He actually put his crummy hands on her, put her on the backburner for his

bastard baby, and somewhat clowned her infertile pussy in

the same instance. What the fuck did she do to deserve

that? As she recalls if she wasn't the recipient of all of her

grandmother's fortunes, then her and Rue's relationship

would be bouncing up and down like a yo-yo right now.

Only thing left to do now was for British to inflict

her pain on other people like she always did. There was no

such thing as godly vengeance to her; she had to handle it

as distress transgressed. British knew exactly where Tia

lived; what kind of girlfriend would she be if she didn't

know the address to her boyfriend's alleged baby mother. It

was time for British to pay Tia a visit to her house whether

Rue was over there or not. It was time for the truth to

finally come out, but first British had to make a quick stop.

Drugstores carried DNA testing kits and it was time for this

verdict to be reached. If Rue was proven not to be the

father of Tia's son, British was going to kill her for wasting Rue's time and disturbing Rue's and British's relationship.

British entered CVS and purchased an at home DNA test, and after purchasing it she threw it inside her purse and made her way to Tia's house. I don't know what made British think Tia was even going to open the door for her, but in her mind it was worth a try. British was going to get some results today and wasn't no way around that. When British pulled up to Tia's house appallingly there wasn't any sign of Rue. British parked, walked up to the porch, and rung Tia's doorbell.

Tia yelled from inside the house, "who is it?"

"It's British," she shouted back.

Tia opened her door fired up. "What reason do you have for coming here today? I'm sure you've seen that Rue isn't here."

"Rue sent me here to swab the baby's mouth. He wants to know once in for all if your son is his or not."

"Your full of shit get the fuck up off my porch and take your raggedy ass home!"

"People who run from DNA tests are proven to be liars. We can do this here and now or we can go to court, and since you have warrants for your arrest I don't think you want to be anywhere near a courthouse."

"So from dusk until dawn all you do is research me? I thought you would've had better things to do like spend your grandmother's money then to do background checks on me and Google me."

"You are a nuisance; a nuisance whose background matters. I don't care what Rue has told you about my personal business concerning my grandmother. I came here for a DNA test and I don't need a rebuttal."

"Who made you the DNA queen? Why isn't Rue present for this? I'm not going to give you my baby's DNA without his father's presence or permission."

"You know I have forbidden him from coming over here until paternity is established. I told him I will be the middle man and I will handle it which is what I'm doing. The quicker we get this over with, the quicker you can get me out of your little hairs. If Rue is the father I will no longer intrude on their relationship."

"Yeah right, your still going to give me a hard time just because that's what you do. Your just not a fair, pleasant person."

"That's not true; I just want to know the truth that's all. You don't have a good track record and I want to know the truth."

"Let's get this over with then come in, but don't make yourself comfortable."

British just entered the front door of Tia's house, but she didn't go any further. All she wanted to do was swab Baby Rhys's mouth or watch Tia swab Baby Rhys's mouth and get gone.

"I'm going to grab Rhys so I guess your going to just stand right there."

"Yep I am."

British reached in her purse and opened the DNA kit to grab one of the swabs for the sample. Tia came back quickly holding Rhys in her arms.

"Give me that cotton thing so I can swab him, I don't want your grimy hands anywhere near my son."

"However you want to do this is fine with me."

Tia snatched the cotton swab and begin circling it around the baby's mouth in urgency so Rhys wouldn't get fussy, but the baby didn't like the feeling of the cotton swab on his tiny jaws so he begin crying.

"I know baby this bitch is about to leave in a few seconds. I know you can probably sense her negative energy, but she is your daddy's sucker friend," Tia begin rocking the baby while British just stood there

"Enough with the foolery and enough swabbing, hand it here," British signaled with her hand open and ready to dip off before she got into a physical altercation. Instead of handing British the swab, Tia threw it at her and it landed on the floor.

"My bad, I guess you got to bend down and pick it up, I mean you always on your knees anyway."

"If you wasn't on your knees sucking Rue's dick and fucking him and other niggas as well, I wouldn't be over here right now getting a DNA test for him, but you been too busy bopping on nigga's dicks to even care about paternity for your child."

Baby Rhys saved Tia's life because British wanted to beat the brakes off of her, but instead she got the last word, she got the cotton swab, put it in her purse, and left. Now British was only missing Rue's sample and of course he was just as headstrong as Tia and he was going to be stubborn about giving DNA as well so British stole some of his DNA. Rue was a cigarette smoker and had loads of cigarette butts in his ashtray so British got a sandwich bag, stuffed her handful in the sandwich bag, and threw it in her package. She went to the nearest UPS location and shipped her package successfully. British couldn't wait for the results to come back so the truth could rear its ugly head. She was about to be checking the mailbox everyday faithfully, and probably beating the mail carrier to the mailbox. She needed those paternity papers just so her and Rue's relationship could mend itself. Hopefully, the results would come back in her favor because if they didn't and Rue didn't shape up, British was going to be as single as a single parent. All British knew was that Tia better not inform Rue about their encounter today. When the DNA results reached her eyes' limits, she was going to tell Rue everything.

Chapter 5: Neck of the Woods

The first prospect, target, slash suspect of Omani's and Onyx's parental wrath was Lindsay's assistant Nestle. Nestle was always clocking hours at Lindsay's headquarters to hold down the fortress. Off rip, Omani knew it wouldn't take any brain power to ambush Lindsay's Eiffel Tower deputy. All the duo had to do was wait for Nestle to exit the building. Once she stepped foot on the streets of the D it was fair game. Looks like Nestle was calling it an early evening by her improbable appearance. It was crunch time now; heels, weapons, and action!

Nestle was headed for her fancy tinted Audi and hadn't hit the unlock button on her key pad as Omani trailed right behind her.

"Hey Nestle!" Omani called out trying to get Nestle to come to a halt.

"Omani is that you?" Nestle questioned the woman gaining on her wondering what in the world could Omani want with her.

"It's me Nestle. You didn't get my invitation?"

"What invitation are you talking about?"

"Tonight you got a date with my trunk." Before Nestle could even think or blink Omani lifted up her right arm and struck Nestle in the back of her head with a sledge hammer knocking her out cold. Onyx put their whip in reverse, backed up in the alley sandwiching Nestle and her car in, flung open the trunk, and threw Nestle inside of it like a garbage bag full of bottles; like pure light mass. Didn't matter if Nestle bumped bodies with the other body in the trunk neither; it would be in her best interest to play sleep even if she wasn't sleep.

Sprinting to the passenger side, Omani hopped in their vehicle and let Onyx pilot the way.

"Stop at the store baby we need to grab a couple of things before we do this."

"What the fuck you mean stop at the store? I'm not stopping at no fucking store! Are you fucking insane? We need to get rid of these got damn bodies before we do anything! Only an idiot would kidnap some people and then go to a fucking store! That's some backwards ass incriminating ass dumb ass shit! What the fuck you been watching World's Dumbest Criminals?"

"First of all, you need to calm down because you sound like a paranoid bitch right now. I didn't think this mission was actually going to work today. I'll go in why you guard the car in case any sudden movements may happen if that's what you worried about, but I doubt it will be any of those. He's dead and she's probably in a coma. While I'm inside the store you can be thinking about a nearby place we can eliminate them at."

"And this is why you don't commit crimes with a woman; you all over the place right now. I can tell this crime shit ain't for you."

"Just take me to Wal-Mart asshole; I ain't trying to hear all that Onyx." Onyx drove Omani to the nearest Wal-Mart hoping that this was going to be the fastest pit stop they had ever made to Wal-Mart. Once inside Wal-Mart Omani sped through the aisles. She retrieved some fishing line, a hair needle, some latex gloves, some rope, some duct tape, some matches, and some lighter fluid." Omani paid for her criminal ingredients with no hastles, exited the store, and seated herself back in the car casually.

"I know exactly how I want to dismantle her and him all I need you to do is pick up those bodies for me. We can set them in the woods."

"I know exactly where we going so get ready."

There was nothing more clandestine then a state park. Edward N.Hines Parkway was the destination; the 20 mile long park passes through the municipalities of Dearborn, Dearborn Heights, Westland, Livonia, Plymouth Township, and Northville Township, MI. That's a six city stretch, which meant six police departments were going to have to open up investigations against the dyad depending on exactly how the felonies they were going to commit massed out. Knowing what they had planned, it was going to be hard for police to catch them up. Rain was coming to wash all or most of any evidence away. Once Onyx and Omani reached the park's perimeters, they rode along the parkway for a split second until they found a low-key spot by some woods where no cars or people seemed to be running or jogging around. Onyx aligned his car fittingly between the yellow lines, straightened his wheel, and backed back so that the trunk would be facing the woods.

Like two grizzly bear's filet mignon, Nestle was trussed to a loose tree log with fishing line. Still unconscious from the Mayweather knockout Omani gave her to the dome, Omani whacked Nestle out of her droopy sleep by toying with a fisherman's hook in and out of her bumpy skin. Those spontaneous hooky motions woke up Nestle painfully so when Omani saw Nestle's red eyes bloom open, Omani yanked the duct tape off of Nestle's mouth like it was a band-aid.

"Why am I in the middle of the wilderness tied to a got damn tree?"

"Sound off bitch and tell me where the fuck is that strait jacket guru you call a boss at with my daughter?"

"I didn't even know you had a daughter Omani. All your hostility shouldn't be directed towards me."

"If you didn't know now you know. I suggest you answer the question before me and my man let you choose your final fate."

"Marcela is the only one who Lindsay shares her location with so why don't y'all go get her and tie her ass up to a tree. Release me!"

"I cannot trust Marcela, she get down with Passive and them."

"I don't see your point. What's wrong with Passive and them? I thought that was your sister?"

"I only got one sister and her name is Kyra so fuck a Smoke and fuck a Passive and since you don't know shit fuck you too!"

"I thought we were better than this Omani. Trees and hostages?"

"You thought wrong, but what you need to consider now is if your mink Brazilian bundles is more important than your sperm bank, catalog ass baby daddy?"

PAUSE:

Nevyn Taylor also known as number 456 in the Cryos International Sperm Bank had a basic, but non-anonymous profile there on file. Nevyn was age 34, hair color black, eye color hazel, mixed with Black and Native American, 6 feet tall, 165lbs, had a Master's Degree in business management and a Bachelor Degree in communications, and was the owner of a popular stock company in Downtown Detroit. Nevyn and Nestle shared a 7-year-old daughter Natalie Alana Parks. When your brother is a captain/cop and you incorporate that with lessons learned from a magazine mastermind you can pretty much find out anything you want to know about anybody. All you need is a computer, the internet, and a credit card. Omani didn't want to involve kids in her violent passage to find Lindsay, because being without her kid was destroying her so instead Omani found someone else she could use for leverage against Nestle. That so happened to be Nevyn. Before Omani and Onyx scooped up Nestle and tossed her ass in the trunk, Omani located Nevyn downtown by his office; she used a computer to hack into his phone and get his GPS to tell her his location. Onyx gunned down on the gas, and they found themselves in another back alley probably by Nevyn's job. When they pulled up on him

Nevyn was grabbing his workbag from his backseat; Onyx

ran out the car, and threw a shoelace around Nevyn's neck

and strangled Nevyn to death. Nevyn was so distraught he

didn't fight back, but he let go of his workbag which fell

back in place in the backseat. I guess he would rather be

killed then robbed. Once Nevyn didn't have a pulse, Omani

popped the trunk open for Onyx to fling his body in it.

Onyx closed Nevyn's door politely so his car didn't look

like it was broken into, hopped right back into the driver's

seat and kept it pushing. Only thing Onyx regretted was

having to kill a man in a suit on a work day.

PLAY:

"How did you find out about that?"

"That's irrelevant; your baby daddy Nevyn is tied to

a log behind you. You can either save yourself or help your

Nevyn get loose so y'all can save each other, but time will

not be of the essence. The end of your fishing line is

threaded to your tracks. It's some straight edge razors

between y'all logs. You better act quickly because it's a lit fire headed towards y'all way."

"What type of jigsaw killer shit is this?" Nestle questioned Omani and Onyx as their backs got further and further away from her stranded eyesight until they disappeared.

Nevyn appeared to still be out cold from whatever visceral defeat he was trying to shake. Little did Nestle know that Nevyn wasn't about to be shaking anything because he was already dead.

"Nevyn! Nevyn! Answer me! I do not want to die here please answer me so we can get out of here!" Nestle pleaded with a dead man smelling smoke and seeing flames.

When her pleads went unanswered Nestle used her back to hit Nevyn's back hoping that their body to body impact would revive him. If only Nestle could see Nevyn's face, she would've been able to see that he was half past dead, but she couldn't.

"This needs to be a collaboration attempt because I'll die quickly if I screw up. Omani is probably counting on me screwing up. That's exactly why she put me in this position with Nevyn. I can't believe somebody made that cock-a-doodle-doo bitch a mother. If I had a penis I wouldn't even tell that vampire bitch I had a penis. She bounces on the dick and the kitty kat and now look at me caught up in the valley of her shit.

"Somebody, anybody help me; I'm almost on fire!" Nestle knew damn well she wasn't going to get no help in these woodlands, but she deserves an E for effort. Remembering she was on the nick of time, Nestle started reaching in between the logs she was fixed too in search of a razor.

"Ouch!"Nestle screamed as she landed a razor in her grip, but she had to stab herself a couple of times just to get it in her hand right. So much for saving baby daddy, but he didn't budge so what was Nestle going to do wait until she was burning like charcoal to try to save herself. How in the hell did Omani find the time or the patience to put fishing line in Nestle's tracks was odd? But killers take all types of provisions to set up their crime scenes and prep their victims. Nestle was trying and trying to get the fishing line out of her tracks, but she just kept cutting her hand and her wrist and cutting the hair. It wasn't like she had a scrunchie or a rubber band to hold the hair up; Nestle had two bundles of weave sewed in her hair on hair weaved onto a fishnet. If Nestle didn't shave herself bald with the razor how in the hell was she going to escape this shit? It was this point in her life she wished she wore wigs, quick weaves, or no weaves.

"Please God, if there is a God help me get out of this!" People never want to call on God until they are in danger in a life or death situation. Nestle should've been praying to God all those years she was working for the devil. She should've been asked God to show her who Lindsay Chambers really was and to remove her from her company in peace.

Where was Lindsay at a time and place like this when Nestle really needed her? Nestle wished she could've told Omani what she wanted to know, but Nestle was telling the truth thus far. She didn't know a damn thing about Lindsay's latest whereabouts. All Nestle could think about was how this was going to be her last memory. Never in her wild mind did she ever think her employer/boss would lead her to her death; a twisted, scary movie, cinema, 21 century death at that.

"This is all this bitch fault; if she wasn't always being shady to people I'll be at home laying on my couch in my bathrobe watching something good off of On-Demand. Unless, I cut myself up some more which is just going to make a bloody mess and cause me more pain, I just got to face that it's no way out of this alive. Bitch, then

killed my baby daddy and now me. Just wait until Lindsay

finds out about this shit because this shit is not going to be

pretty for Omani or her crack head looking ass nigga." The

fire was getting nearer and nearer; Nestle could smell it,

she could sense it, she could feel the heat of it, and she

could see it even though she closed her eyes and tried not to

look. Before she knew it she was flambéed like a gourmet

dish and she didn't bother to scream as much as the fire

charbroiled her clothes, her skin, and her body to the core.

This fire was worst then childbirth, or being surgically

operated on while alive, it was no comparable pain like it.

Only thing Nestle could think of comparing it to was hell.

The fire spread quickly from the shoes on her feet up to the

weave on her skull and wiped her out completely. Before

she was dead she just asked God to protect her daughter

now that she was going to be without a mother or father.

Chapter 6: Sweet Dreams and Kerosene

Nodding off into a somber sleep, Paradise picked the wrong time and place to take a catnap. Cahill's house was not her house anymore and this was going to be the last day she laid in his bed. Her time in his life was expired and nobody exited his life in one peace, shape, or form. As she slept in a t-shirt with no panties on, he dumped out his suspicious grocery bag. Luckily, she was sleep on her back so he spread her legs open like he was about to penetrate her dreams. Instead he poured lighter fluid all over her vagina. Cahill predicted Paradise must've had her daily round of Cranberry Mimosas so she wasn't going to budge easily. He took this as his leverage over her to destroy her just for thinking she could play him like a poo-putt. Since he had another woman named Cabella her presence was no longer needed and she could get the fuck on with what she started with when she met him since she would rather be with a lame ass bodyguard then a mayor.

Unlike most men who felt like both parties should suffer, Cahill was different. You can't blame a nigga for being a nigga and thinking with his dick because he has two heads, but you can blame a bitch for being a bitch because she only has one head. Cahill didn't want to do anything to Rock and he didn't have too because the way he was going to leave Paradise was payback enough.

Cahill made sure the lighter fluid container was as empty as a dry well. He shook it upside down a couple of times to make sure it didn't have any more drops in it. Nothing else came out so he just dropped it onto the floor. He took his pack of matches and struck a match and threw it on her honey pot. Her pussy began to simmer, fester, and smoke like sirloin on a BBQ grill. Cahill gawked at Paradise thinking for a minute. "That's what you get you useless bitch," and then he wiped his hands off and left his house to smolder into ashes.

Darting up smelling smoke and feeling a humid, burning sensation, Paradise looked down and saw baby sparks and flames rising from the bed.

"Oh my God! What the fuck has he done! My vagina is on fire! My fucking vagina is on fire!"

Springing up, Paradise ran to the bathroom, turned the cold water knob on high and began making a tub full of water. Next, she turned on the bathroom sink and began splashing water everywhere tryna put the fire out in between her firebox. The bathtub was taking forever to fill up; Paradise kept splashing water everywhere like it was a water park in the bathroom. The fire was dying down, but her vagina was suffering. Paradise jumped in the tub and soaked her kitty kat. She formed the ugliest bathtub water color ever that looked worst then a ring of dirt around the tub.

Entering the house Rock smelled char. He knew it was something wrong.

"Paradise? Where you at my baby?"

"I'm in the tub!"

"What the fuck happened here so fast?"

"He set my vagina on fire; he mine as well had just set me on fire instead."

"If he can't have you I guess nobody can."

"How in the fuck am I supposed to explain this shit when I'm trying to be admitted into the hospital, Hi, my name is Paradise Rice and my vagina just got set on fire; can you check it out and see what's left of it for me."

"I know this is crazy baby, but the shit could be worse. Your lucky to even be sitting here with me right now and talking to me as I am the same. Put your pride aside and get dressed so we can go to the hospital. I'm here for you, no matter what happens. No matter what the doctor says or anybody says, I'm here strictly for you."

"Do you plan on pressing charges on him for this?"

"Why would I press charges on him so he can call his friends at the police headquarters and shred my case up? I'm not wasting my time doing that bullshit."

"And you don't have to I'm going to get that son of a bitch for this shit just watch me."

$

Out with the old and in with the new; Cahill's new flame was an enticing 26-year-old pink headed Detroit weather reporter whose name was Cabella Ross. Cabella had all men especially Cahill fiending for her every time she gave a weather report so he sent her fancy gifts from every Somerset Mall store you could think of. Gladly, Cabella would send every gift back with a different sarcastic note. For example, Cahill sent Cabella some Versace perfume; Bright Crystal fragrance so Cabella sent the perfume back with a note that said, "I love this scent and I just copped me a bottle of it so keep probing." Another note said, "thank you, but no thank you; I don't accept gifts from men." Cahill was astounded because no woman had ever turned down his gifts. The first time Cahill received a gift back from Cabella marked the moment that Cahill begin to question Paradise as a woman and every woman he had ever dated. After three months of clever rejection, Cabella finally agreed to let Cahill take her out and every since their first date the two have been indivisible.

It was so many positive traits to Cahill's new obsession with Cabella. First of all, Cabella had pride and that domineering pride reminded him of his goddaughter Passive. Cabella was financially independent and a hustle bunny unlike the lazy bitch he had sitting in his house terrified of her own enemies. Why wasn't Paradise plotting against her enemies? Why wasn't Paradise reassessing the women she claimed to be haunting her because Paradise was currently irrelevant to both Lindsay and Passive? Of course her past stunts weren't forgotten or forgiven, but she had time to enjoy some life. Why wasn't Paradise trying to find a new hustle or a new connect? Why was Paradise so content with living off of other people's hard-earned money?

At first, Cahill thought that he could runoff in the moonlight with Paradise so he tried to stay true to that belief by loving her and shielding her, but he was wrong. Cabella's fine ass snapped Cahill back into his standards. He should've left Paradise to rot in Missouri with her thievery and end up dead like her home girl Champagne.

Chapter 7: Pass the Throne

Wasn't no mountain high enough for Mrs. Lindsay

Chambers because that's exactly where she was stationary.

She was near the Huron Mountains up in the Upper

Peninsula in Marquette, Michigan. Lindsay guessed the

bird brain Mitchells' would least expect her to even remain

in Michigan or flee to Northern Michigan.

People who resided in the mountains don't know

shit about all the other regions of Michigan; all they know

is their city and that's what they put on for. None of these

upper Michiganders would know that they were in the

presence and vicinity of a DSM-5 accredited sociopath.

Amory Mitchell whose last name was renamed too

Chambers was now three-months-old and even though

babies know the difference between their parents and

strangers, she was fully adjusted to her baby-snatching, evil

stepmother. Amory was full of smiles, babbles, upper

strength, and many other three-month-old milestones. Often

Lindsay went inside the nursery to check on Amory even though she had a full-time nanny. Nobody was too be trusted with baby Amory.

As Lindsay walked in the pink and black cheetah print nursery she heard camera, telephone snaps. Apparently, her nanny Charlotte was taking selfies with Amory and kissing Amory like they was up under a mistletoe or some shit. Lindsay's rules were simple; no pictures, and absolutely no kissing on the baby.

"The fuck is wrong with bitches; I pay this bitch 2,000 a week to be a fucking nanny not a photographer or a human kissing bug. I know Amory is a fucking Gerber baby, but my rules are my rules."

Just as Lindsay was about to get in gear to dispose of Charlotte, someone was rudely pressing the buzzard at her security gate aimlessly.

"Stop hitting the buzzard like a maniac!" Lindsay hollered through the intercom system letting British in.

"Just avoiding any drive-bys you know how we Chambers get down."

"Ain't nobody going to find us out here I tell you that much."

Seems like British and Lindsay were now Batman and Robin; they were family mine as well stick together. Being shady was their favorite commodity and one shady mission always led to the electricity of another and another.

"So British I asked you to come up here because I want to pass my torch too you. Your younger than me, your faster than me, and you are more invisible then me. When it's time for me to return I will, but right now I'm gonna work through you."

"Lindsay, I appreciate the offer, but I got my own problems brewing right now."

"What type of shady bitch are you? Shady bitches don't have problems."

"You're wrong about that; everybody has problems people just deal with them differently."

"I'll help you with your problems if you take my torch and by that I mean going after the entire Mitchell family. I'm talking about Passive, Smoke, Omani, Onyx, the 11th precinct, Kyra, Andrea, Andre, even my own sister Marcela. I got something for every single one of them and this is a one-man job. You got what it takes to see all my missions through. I say you got a 100% probability because not many people can get away with kidnapping a baby out of a hospital and making it this far without getting caught. You don't have any enemies; just think about the death of my mother Liz Chambers and our relative Novara Chambers. Are you going to sit back and let those Mitchells' wipeout our family like a grenade?"

"No, I'm not; I'll take your throne, just don't be mad at me when I'm better at what you do then you."

"Okay, but look I need you to watch Amory for me right quick I'm about to run outside and do something."

"I'll watch her no problem where is she?"

"She's inside her nursery. You know I don't like people all up in her face so just walk in there and check on her every couple of minutes."

"You got it cuz."

Running outside Lindsay grabbed a shovel and began digging a hole on her 4,700 square foot property. She was throwing dirt back like she was a pro-gardener. Somebody was about to get buried.

She went back in the house and found Charlotte patrolling near Amory's nursery. Lindsay asked Charlotte to meet her outside by the hole in the ground. Immediately, Charlotte became goose-bumpy because the look that Lindsay gave her was to die for.

Charlotte didn't know what the hell she was about to do to escape this one, but she was definitely about to take her chances using 4,700 square feet to help her flee, before she cooperated into standing by a manhole. Something wasn't right about Lindsay Chambers' and Charlotte's conscious told her to leave now and to take the baby with her for leeway.

While Lindsay was outside waiting, Charlotte grabbed Amory out of her crib, swiftly snuck past British without being noticed and exited the front door as silently as she could. She treaded to her vehicle, fastened Amory in her nanny car-seat, got in, and slammed her foot on the gas. Expeditiously, she entered her security code on the security keypad and exited Lindsay's house like a fire truck exits a firehouse. Lucky for Charlotte her engine was quiet too; she mine as well be invincible.

Charlotte's heart was pounding so high-speed while she was driving, she was scared it was going to pop out her chest and hit the steering wheel. What was she going to do now and where was she going to go? So much for having a job; there goes next week's pay and the week after that and the week after that. Charlotte was just going to have to figure everything out as it came. Long as she was safe from Lindsay that was all that mattered. Charlotte checked her rearview mirror and made sure Amory was okay. Amory was sleeping like most babies do her age strapped in her car-seat.

Once it felt like Lindsay was waiting on Charlotte far too long, she entered the house asking questions.

"Have you seen Charlotte?" Lindsay questioned British.

"I told that broad I was looking for her and to come outside."

"I haven't seen her none since I've been here."

"Have you been checking the nursery like I asked you too?"

"I was just about to get up and check on Amory before you came in here with your foot up your ass."

Lindsay ran to Amory's nursery to find that Amory was missing. Something told Lindsay to check the vehicles in the driveway next. It was only two vehicles in the drive which meant one was missing and Amory was missing.

"This bitch then stole my baby!"

"Technically she's not your baby Lindsay."

"Shut the fuck up and help me think. How do I steal a baby back I stole? How do I report a baby missing that's already been reported missing?"

"What makes you think Charlotte isn't coming back and didn't just take Amory with her to run some errands?"

"I didn't give that trick no errands to run. I was about to kill her and I think she knew I was about to kill her and took off with Amory. Her life would've lasted longer if she didn't kidnap Amory, but now she got to die off. I'm talking on some stray bullet sniper shit."

"What could a nanny possibly do wrong to make you want to kill her?"

"I have house rules that have to be followed and she broke two rules. No kissing the baby and no photographs with the baby."

"I mine as well be starring in a movie on Lifetime."

"You mine as well go find Charlotte and Amory before we both go down."

"You go find Amory, since you want to play mommy so bad; that's your child. I'm going to go start terrorizing people instead."

"British come on," Lindsay yawned.

"Lindsay, all jokes aside you looking real pale right now, your skin is super dry, and you just yawned after attempting to kill someone. The Lindsay I know is never tired so tell me what's going on?"

"Okay I've been feeling a little off lately and I think I missed my period and I've been pissing like a drunk."

"Bitch, you pregnant, but if you are pregnant I don't know who you can be pregnant by."

"The only man I ever slept with is Smoke."

"Bitch please, somebody else been knocking them boots. You and Smoke haven't been together in years."

"We had lots of sex at the cabin."

"How you goin impregnate yourself using your own hostage? That's just sick."

"Take me to get a pregnancy test before we make any more assumptions."

"Where the fuck is a pharmacy at around these boondocks because it ain't nothing, but land and water around here?"

Sure enough Lindsay tried to find the closest pharmacy to her house and there wasn't no nearby CVS pharmacy; it was only off brand pharmaceutical companies and Walgreen's. According to GPS, Walgreen's was 37 minutes away with light traffic so British did her best to follow directions and not to get turned around. When Lindsay and British made it to Walgreen's and made it to the aisle for the expected/unexpected mothers, she teased Lindsay some more.

"What you want lines, words, or smiley faces?"

"Just pick one or two damn, stop making this so difficult."

Soon as they purchased the pregnancy tests it was back to the car. Lindsay didn't feel like sitting in one spot with a seatbelt on for half an hour again especially when her bladder was liable to make her pee again, but she had to in order to get back home.

With the help of GPS navigation, British was making their way back to Lindsay's undercover palace.

"So what are you going to do about Charlotte now?"

"If I'm truly pregnant fuck Charlotte and Amory, Her daddy can go fetch his daughter."

"I'm lost."

"Don't try to figure the shit out because it's a long story just drive."

British and Lindsay wasn't even halfway home yet and Lindsay had to pee badly.

"Pull over I gotta pee."

"Hold it."

"I can't hold it you better pull this thing over now before I do."

"Like your boogey ass is really about to pop a squat and piss on a local freeway."

"I'm not joking, give me a couple napkins, give me a pregnancy test, and be my lookout."

"Who the hell takes a pregnancy test on the side of the road? A baby mother test should be taken in the privacy of your own home or a medical facility. I hope you use your night vision and you don't miss the stick."

"Shut up British!"

Before Lindsay opened up her passenger door she opened up the box to pregnant life. British's self-righteous ass didn't even open up the box or explain the directions on how to use it. British probably never took a pregnant test before either, but hell she should've been paying attention for when her day came. Lindsay skimmed through the piss directions, now it was time for her to let it rip. Within seconds she was pissing on stick number one and relieved her bladder for awhile. She wiped her cooch with the napkins and pulled her leggings up anxious to know the results. Soon as Lindsay got back in the car the results was in; she was PREGGO.

"I'm pregnant."

"Oh my God what are you going to do now?"

"I'm going to have this baby, duh. I'm going to screenshot this shit to him right now."

Lindsay just had to tell Smoke the good news about their unborn child. As far as she knew, she was going to be the first woman to have Smoke's child she had no idea that Passive was pregnant. His own wife couldn't even do that which is exactly why Smoke should've just married Lindsay in the first place. Lindsay screenshot her pregnancy stick with the two positive lines on it in the positive box and texted it to Smoke with the tagline we're pregnant with the signature Mrs. Chambers.

Smoke just so happened to be scrolling through the internet on his phone when the text message icon flew across his screen. Curiously, he clicked on it and read the message. He almost had a heart attack after reading what it said.

"I really hope she's playing mind games with me, please let her be playing mind games." Smoke knew if Passive found out Lindsay was pregnant, she was really going to be walking out the hospital doors in a heartbeat and nobody was going to be able to stop her or talk to her not even Smoke. He was just going to have to keep this a secret until he could find someone who he could make a plan of action with, but no matter what Passive could never know about this. This had to be a mistake, a prank, a text message mistap or something.

Chapter 8: Game Changers

It was like tombstones in a cemetery for Passive to be opening up her eyes to the dead walls of a hospital until Smoke entered into her room.

"Smoke, when are they going to discharge me? I need them to discharge me today."

"Your worried about all the wrong things right now love. You need to worry about our unborn child and only our unborn child."

"We might be expecting, but we still have business to tend too. Expectant mothers work until their head-on with their delivery date."

"That's them; they ain't registered to this room right now under a 24-hour microscope facing a high-risk pregnancy you are and you are by far a free-spirit. We have too many enemies for you to turn our unborn child into a wager."

"I understand all of that, but I still have a few family duties. Baby please don't limit me now."

"You are not going after Cahill and you sure as hell aren't going after Lindsay. Rock, Elvia, and I promise you that we'll be watching you so don't do nothing sly because you will be redirected every time.

"What do you mean Rock is going to be watching me? When did that come about? Who decided that?"

"It's only temp until he flees town."

"Y'all two fools were just fighting right; I'm lost, but I got things to do. I'm about to go handle my business." Passive proceeded to sit up straight, turn to the side of her hospital bed dropping her footie feet to the floor and rise up.

"I will make them strap you down Passive please just chill out and sit this one out."

"Why are you doing this to me Smoke?"

"Our pregnancy is high-risk; you have to stay in the hospital until the baby comes out or else you will lose the baby."

"Just give me an abortion then; this baby ain't going to kill me or us." Smoke couldn't his ear waves. Clearly, his wife needed to get her hormones together. He dropped his guard and opted to leave the room without even catching a glimpse of Passive. They finally are on the verge of becoming parents and Passive is acting like killing people is more important than motherhood.

"How could she be so selfish when its women paying racks to even conceive a baby and here Passive is not appreciating her blessing?"

Passive knew that she had pissed off her husband because he had never, ever turned his back on her before when they were having a discussion.

I don't know what he's mad for; ain't like he got to spend a century in a fucking hospital like a medical rat or something. As much money as we got we can pay for a house doctor. I can sit on bed-rest at home. He knows I got a phobia for hospitals so why is he letting them imprison me? Our unfinished business is important because it ultimately affects our present and our future. What will happen if one of our enemies get close to me? Can't nobody protect me at a hospital and I will not let Lindsay, Omani, or Cahill or anybody else out there hurt my baby or me. If only Passive knew all the things that Smoke was juggling on his plate right now outside of her and the baby, she would've probably been more compassionate towards him.

As Passive was thinking she started yawning and decided to stay put and take a nap.

Smoke on the other hand was still livid and went to go confide in Elvia.

Smoke shot Elvia a text before he left the hospital parking arena.

What's your location Elvia?

At my house.

I'm about to come through. I need to vibe with you real quick about Passive.

Come on then bro you know you are welcome.

On the way.

Once Smoke reached Elvia's place he couldn't wait to vent to her. So much was going through his brain about Passive and the baby. She was like a totally different woman to him now that she was hospitalized and expecting.

Smoke entered Elvia's house like it was business as usual.

"Make yourself at ease," Elvia told Smoke.

"Let me get some water or something; my mouth is going to be dry after I finish yapping to you because I got a lot to say."

"Talk on that's what I'm here for."

"I honestly think that Passive wishes she wasn't pregnant. I don't know how to tame the non-pregnant Passive with the pregnant Passive. Our personal and business relationship is intertwining and I don't know which one to choose sides with. Passive just wants to be Diamond and I want her to just be Passive."

"You helped create Diamond so you can't get mad that Diamond wants to rein things."

"I know I did, but she's pregnant. What type of man would I be to let my pregnant wife mob people like it ain't pregnant women getting babies cut out of them and mutilated every day? I don't want that to be Passive and that is my biggest fear."

"Passive is a different breed of woman. Why don't you trust her as your wife and your business partner?"

"Trust is not the question; new life is the variable here. I don't want her doing nothing that jeopardizes her life or the baby's life."

"That's like telling a hustler he can't hustle no more Smoke. Y'all just goin have to keep bumping heads Smoke. You just got to rock with it otherwise you goin push her away."

"Okay, but that's just one thing I have something else to tell you."

"Lindsay has reached out to me from whatever mountain cliff she is on and claims to be pregnant with my baby." Elvia leaped up from her seat because Smoke hit a nerve with his punk ass confession.

"What the fuck you mean Smoke? You had sex with that serpent willingly and raw?"

"She kidnapped me and stole sex from me. What could I do I was tied up? "

"If your dick came and it stayed hard that means you liked it, No matter how tied up you was you could've controlled your dick right, but I guess not when it's being slid up into some pussy. You let yourself come into some rotten pussy who knows how many times?"

"Stop focusing on the sex, we need to worry about this baby, if it is a baby."

"How about we just start planning your funeral because Passive is going to kill you and you know it."

"Passive isn't going to kill me because she's never going to find out about this. We are going to find Lindsay and kill her."

"Now you killing babies Smoke? I'm just learning everything about you today so what else are you hiding?"

"Are you down for this or should have I just kept my mouth shut?"

"I really want to fire on your ass right now Smoke because this shit is messy and bold business. You don't fuck your enemies with a hard dick; you slit their throat with a cold knife. If you can't hold a knife you stick a razor blade up under your tongue. You do something so you can always defend yourself. I'm doing this for Passive not you because I ain't got time for her to be crying on my couch about you."

"She's not going to cry about me, I'll never let her shed a tear because of me or make a tear even form in her gorgeous green eyes. I see you feel some type of way so I'm just going to leave before your veins pop out any more at me. I want you and Posh to get a lead on where Lindsay is. You don't have to do it for me, do it for Passive."

On that note, Smoke left the premises and even though Elvia wanted to slaughter Smoke for allegedly impregnating his psycho ex-girlfriend Lindsay who had to be dealt with ASAP. Elvia had to put Posh on board because she couldn't take any chances of dealing with

Lindsay alone. A report would get more recognition with two missing people then a report with one missing person.

"How in the hell are we going to find this crooked bitch?" Posh asked Elvia clueless as to where their trail was going to begin.

"Doesn't she have an office somewhere Downtown?"

"Yeah, that was good thinking. Let's find her office, I'm sure it has got to be some clues there."

"Do your magic and find it then." Elvia was the computer whiz out the group at least whenever Smoke and Passive weren't around she was. She pinpointed Lindsay's office using her tablet and made their way to the Penobscot Building. Elvia and Posh just so happen to end up in the same back alley as Nestle's car- a silver Audi. They had to find a way to skip out of paying for parking because parking in Downtown Detroit was always pricey even for a 30 minute trip. They parked behind it, crossed the streets, and entered into the building searching for the right elevators that went up to floor 31. Once an elevator was free, they boarded the elevators, and looked for the Dirty Raw sign on the wall. After, they found that sign, they tried the door, and to their surprise it wasn't locked. Once they got inside, they hit the lights and begin skimming through cabinets, draws, boxes, and closets pretty much everything in reach and sight. They came across some leasing papers for properties that Lindsay owned in Marquette, Michigan. The leasing papers had Lindsay's name on them as the leaser and the properties were each one year old then the other. On the office desk, they noticed it was a picture of a young lady standing by a silver Audi that resembled the same car they parked behind outside, and a gold plated sign that read Nestle Parks (assistant).

"Assistant huh? I can't phantom how anybody can work for that derelict bitch. Where the hell is this assistant Nestle Parks? Her car is parked outside," Posh wondered.

"I don't think she could be here otherwise it would've been some lights on, but that could explain why the door was open. She must've planned on coming back."

"All I know is this the only chance we got to find some dirt on Lindsay and we're getting somewhere, but I know we can find more stuff if we look a little longer."

"If we gotta ice her then we gotta ice her because it's our mission to find Lindsay."

After searching some more, Posh and Elvia found Public Storage papers for a storage unit in Farmington Hills.

"I wonder what this bitch got stored up in her unit."

"Those storage places have cameras and codes galore everywhere. We're not going to be able to get up in there."

"We can do anything we put our mind too, but let's go before somebody finds us. We should probably check old girl car when we get outside too. That's if it's still there; she could've been exiting the building as we were entering the building."

"Your right that could be the case."

Departing the building, Posh and Elvia back-tracked their trail to their vehicle and Nestle's fancy car was still sitting there lonely and vacant as hell.

"You try the door," Elvia directed Posh.

"Shut your scary ass up, the worst thing that could happen is the alarm going off.

"This is an Audi; this thing probably got 10 alarms in one, and some other type of security technology shit we don't even know about. I'm not touching the door, you touch it, just be ready to jump in the car and pull off."

Posh touched the doors to the silver, tinted Audi, and the doors were still unlocked. Looking inside she wondered who in the hell would leave an Audi unattended in Downtown Detroit with the doors unlocked. It wasn't any blood inside of it, but it was a purse sitting on the passenger side under the glove department. Posh checked the purse and there was all of Nestle's information; driver's license, social security card, credit cards, cash, and more. Something was definitely wrong with this picture because wouldn't no sane person leave a Audi stranded with a fully intact Givenchy purse sitting inside of it..

"Whoever this Nestle girl is, she must be missing," Posh hypothesized.

"Well that's too bad for her; people go missing every day. Our concern is Passive so get your nosey ass in the car so we can go."

"Finding her has a big chance of leading us directly to Lindsay. Assistants know everything and since she's clearly been running the office while Lindsay is sheltering herself from the world. She knows everything we need to know."

"Don't be stupid ain't nobody driving no Audi or carrying no Givenchy bag about to snitch on they boss."

"I'm not about to waste any of my time finding her

so if you want too you can get the fuck out and do that shit

yourself. Otherwise, I'm going to use what we got, share

this ammo we found with Smoke and keep it pushing."

Chapter 9: Racy

So many thoughts were racing inside of Omani's head, but her gas pedal refused to stop accelerating. She still had a lot of work to do in the lives of all the shysters that stood between her and Amory reuniting.

Remembering that Passive and Smoke were kidnapped in or somewhere near Missouri, Omani theorized that would be their next destination. She was sure she would uncover some of her ex brother's and sister's skeletons. It had to be somebody who wanted to retaliate against the duo just as much as Omani did. Omani had better be careful because Lindsay didn't have shit on the tree barks she was going up in Missouri.

Since Grant was the closest relative in Missouri Omani could think of she figured she would pay him a visit.

"Where are we headed to Omani?"

"Why don't you just navigate? I'll tell you where you go and you just drive there."

"So am I your man or your navigator because I thought we were calling the shots together."

"Why can't you just have my back? Clearly, this is not one of our submissive times we use to."

"I got a bad feeling about us being in Missouri. Both Passive and Smoke were kidnapped in this town. What makes you think we're going to make it out safe and sound?"

"So what you got on panties now? We just killed two people. You should've left your chicken heartedness in the forest with them."

"The last thing you should want is for our journey to get derailed here."

"Grow some balls, we're going over my cousin Grant house to see what he knows."

Through newfound tension, the two O's made it securely to Grant's house. Omani exited the vehicle to bang on Grant's door.

"What's the password?"

"It's your cousin Omani now open up!"

"I know you didn't just say Omani?"

"I did."

Grant hurried up and opened the door because didn't no fam ever come visit him. At least nobody other than Smoke.

"Give me a hug girl where's Smoke?"

"Smoke is back home, he couldn't come, but he told me to send you his helloes. He's in a do not disturb status if you know what I mean," Omani lied.

"I ain't been in the communicating mood myself since Chill got locked up. This is the first time me and my brother ever been separated. This shit is for the birds so you down here with who and why?"

"I'm traveling with my baby daddy and we're searching for my daughter. Lindsay kidnapped her from the hospital right after I gave birth somehow."

"That degenerate bitch working her way down the family tree!"

"Please tell me you know something that can help me get to Lindsay."

"Lindsay is both Passive's and Smoke's forte. I know two people who betrayed Smoke for Lindsay and one of those people is dead."

"So what about the other one?"

"Her name Paradise and word around town is Cahill Caesar is her boyfriend. I don't know how you goin get to her she heavily guarded."

"I'm lost who is Cahill Caesar?"

"Girl how do you live somewhere and you didn't even know who your own mayor was? I know Smoke taught you better than that. You too street savvy not to know who this cat is; he is the mayor here, he use to be the mayor in Detroit, but I guess they exiled him from y'all state now he then landed here. He is supposed to be Passive's god dad and her father's best friend. He has a lot of history with Passive's family."

This was the most glorious news Omani could've got out of her first rat. Passive's god dad? That would be the foremost cunning way to get back at Passive for being an accessory to kidnapping then we all could be even. Since Omani lost somebody, Passive has to lose somebody too. Omani was brave as hell, how she figured she could just come to somebody's state and wipeout their mayor especially when she didn't even know the real pretenses that stood between Cahill and Passive or Cahill and Lindsay.

"Well I need to be going my baby daddy is outside waiting."

"You sure you don't need me to handle that for you. You know how I get done?"

"Smoke and Passive got it, you just sit this one out. I'll keep your offer in mind though in case we should need you."

Just as Grant was overseeing Omani to the passenger side of Onyx's vehicle, they were blocked by a gang of intruders. Onyx was surrounded by a bunch of soundless bikes whose silver parts and handle bars still gleamed and glistened at night. Their lights were shutoff like DTE cut the power source on the whole neighborhood. No engines were humming and all bodies were still.

"Who the fuck is y'all cuz?" Grant demanded.

"We just want her and him. You can go back into that shabby shack you call a house bro before we torque your ass too."

"Gab is that you? Remembering him and his motorcycle club from an old family reunion, Omani singled him out.

"Ain't nobody here named Gab. We caught y'all little amateur forest charade killing two people, but it's over 50 in this squad so how y'all goin handle that?"

"Ain't nobody about to kidnap nobody in front of my got damn house!"

"It's over 50 of us out here so don't be fucking stupid bro! Soon as you turn your back one of my guys will launch a bullet through your back if you don't walk away from this. We got beef with Smoke. These two motherfuckers probably came here to ice your ass, like I said they just killed two people up in a forest so get the fuck on while you can!"

"Damn they savages cuz take they asses away," Grant played it off to see how far he could get before he grabbed his two burners he hid outside of his house or if he could actually make it into his house so he could give Smoke the rundown." Grant just wanted to make it in his house because if he were to shoot off blazing bullets, he would be slaughtered because he was too outnumbered.

"I thought you would see things my way. Get your pretty ass over here Omani. We goin have so much fun with your bubble ass tonight." Omani was beginning to feel like shit and wish that she wouldn't have been so freaking stubborn and hard-headed. Who in the hell was goin rescue her now? She said fuck both Smoke and Passive in the same damn token and the Monarchs weren't bullshitting Grant, he turned his back and made it into his house without one single bullet or wound.

Grant sprung to his phone to call Smoke.

"Grant talk to me bro."

"I know you in do not disturb status, but this is urgent."

"I'm not in no fucking do not disturb status who the fuck told you that?"

"Your sister Omani did. What motorcycle gang do you got beef with?"

"She back to her old gimmicks. I thought that shit was dead, but I guess you talking about Gab and The Monarchs."

"Well your sister just came to visit me and they just kidnapped her and her baby daddy right outside my house."

"What the fuck was the Monarchs doing in Missouri and what the fuck was Omani doing in Missouri?"

"Your sister ain't in good shape at all. They say your sister and her baby daddy just killed two people in a forest. She was fishing for info about your enemies."

"What the fuck man I don't have time for this shit right now. Passive is pregnant on bed-rest, my niece has been kidnapped, and now Onyx and Omani have been kidnapped too. Can I get a fucking break?"

"If it's anything I can do I got you. I will be on the next flight to Michigan. I'm surprised they even let me go."

"You can't trust them or whatever they told you because I thought this beef was dead, but I see this beef is still alive. I hope this is not the last time I talk to you, but whatever you do watch your back as you see they some wily, shady motherfuckers."

"You gone and get back to Passive and we'll brainstorm how to get Omani home-free tomorrow."

"That sounds like a plan remember what I said Grant."

Grant was wrong, nobody let him go. When he was standing outside watching his cousin, and her baby daddy get abducted, somebody hid themselves in his house. They were just waiting long enough for Grant to deliver the message to Smoke in the exact time manner he did. He would've been better off fleeing his house and calling

Smoke, but in his case you live and you learn or you live and then you die and his time was up.

Grant was showering in his bathroom when one of the Monarchs slid open his glass shower door on him and shot him in the head. He died instantly, he mines as well had of went out in a blazing glory instead of dying a sucker ass death. If only he would've had enough time to reach the gun he had planted in the back of the toilet he might still be alive.

$

Lindsay's mysterious pregnancy was driving Smoke crazy; but knowing that Elvia and Posh had his back was taking a little pressure off of his mind. When he reviewed the girls' findings he couldn't believe that Lindsay was so damn close to them still.

"This bitch gotta be in upper Michigan especially if these papers were found at her office. She must've had made some present use of them. She probably had Nestle

making her house payments for her. Lindsay be hiding her money in all types of accounts and Nestle always assisted Lindsay at everything."

"I want y'all to go check this rental space out in Marquette, go ask questions, go show pictures, let's see what her neighbors know, and don't stop until you find her."

"We got you Smoke, we're going to terrorize the UP," Elvia stated.

"I just got one question Smoke," Posh asked Smoke.

"What is it?"

"How much do you know about her assistant Nestle?"

"Shut up Posh, I thought that shit was dead."

"It is dead, but this Nestle chick is missing."

"I'm sure she is missing look who her boss is. When an enemy strikes they strike at everybody around you. We know way too much about that."

"Both of y'all are taking this for a joke, but its okay just wait. Y'all are going to see that this girl being missing is connected to us somehow."

"

"

Chapter 10: Partum

Tia's body was starting to reject new motherhood. She was so withdrawn from herself she couldn't even formulate a reaction that somebody was threatening the livelihood of her son. She didn't even have one ounce of rebuttal in her; it was buried by this post condition overtaking her. By the day Tia was becoming more dangerous to herself and her son. Thank goodness, Rue visited his son on the regular, because if he didn't he would've flicked on the news and his baby's mother and son would be the subject of a breaking story.

A mother can hear and feel their child crying even in the deepest level of sleep. It was time for another feeding and Rhys was crying uncontrollably. His cries got louder and louder like he added bass in his cries still Tia didn't budge. Rhys kept crying hoping for that nice, warm bottle his mother always swayed him with when he was hungry and finally Tia woke up. She heard Rhys crying and yelled, "shut the fuck up and go back to sleep!" She pulled the covers over her head and stuffed a pillow over her face like that was actually going to quiet a screaming baby.

"I swear this baby was the biggest mistake in my life! Why didn't I just get an abortion at the clinic like any other dumb pregnant bitch who got pregnant for the wrong reasons? It's nothing cute about a baby! From carrying it, birthing it, and now raising it; this baby has got to go."

Tia hopped up and stomped to Rhys' room where she grabbed one of his stuffed animals, applied lots of pressure, and began to suffocate him like he was a grown man. It had been a minute and Tia was still suffocating him. She was in the zone; she didn't hear Rue creeping in. He always went straight to Rhys' room before even acknowledging Tia because his son was the only bond that mattered to him in that house anything else was inefficient.

Rue ran to Rhys and pushed Tia far away from his crib. "What the fuck are you doing to my son bitch?"

"You can leave part time baby daddy. Don't worry about me and Rhys because we good. We don't need you and we never needed you."

The baby was so cold and blue. "Shut the fuck up you killed my son? How could you kill my firstborn child and my only son? This baby was the only thing you was good for bitch. Other then that I wish I could reverse your ass back to start where I would've left you hanging at. This is exactly why you don't fuck an ordinary bitch raw."

"All you care about is British; that bitch ain't never ever been to no Britain let alone no foreign country."

"It's something seriously wrong with you; your mental institutional dysfunctional. I'm going yo call the mental hospital police and the 911 police ASAP."

"I don't care who you call! Call them! Call every got damn number in your phone book until your battery dies. Don't make me no difference."

Quickly, still with Rhys in his arms, Rue called 911 and told them they were dealing with an erratic moron who just suffocated her son to death in his crib. Police cars were zooming down Lawton Street in a fast responsive time. Police cars are always accompanied by ambulances so that was right on time. First thing first, police arrested Tia in reference to the 911 call labeling her the assailant. Next objective was to take the baby from Rhys so his body could go to the morgue and have a proper burial, but Rhys didn't want to let go.

"I know this is a tragedy young man, but you have to turn the baby over into our custody," a heavyset officer insisted.

"Yesterday my son was still breathing now look at him today. I guess it's some sense in why they say it's hard for a woman to raise a man."

"I'm sorry for your loss, we are all sorry for your loss, but it's time to say goodbye to your son." Silently,

Rue told his son that he loved him and may he rest in heaven.

"I hope y'all give that bitch the death penalty because if y'all don't I'll find me an insider to see the job through."

"The law is the most practical method of justice so let the lawyers and prosecutors and judges who are going to be handling this case do their job." Just like that Rhys was pronounced dead by alleged suffocation and any other identification of foul play was being left to the microscope to determine. Rue had no idea how he was going to cope with losing his son or how he was going to run all this down to British without her getting pleasure and joy out of Tia being a fuck-up and being able to fulfill Rue's paternal bond.

As a matter of fact, Rue figured he should just skip town for awhile. He was no use to anybody in his current mind frame. Fuck all women right now; it was time for him to get ghost, hit the airport, and pick a spot to travel too. Who knows where he would end up, but long as it wasn't anywhere near the usual.

$

While all the disorder was levitating at Tia's house, at British's house was finally her moment of deliberation. The mailman had finally put that golden letter in her mailbox that was going to shed light on everything. Omani ripped open the letter seal like it was an income tax check she was about to go to the bank and cash. According to the DNA findings, Rue WAS 99.9% THE FATHER of Tia's baby. British hurled the letter down pissed off that she was wrong about her and now she had to respect Tia's link to Rue.

"I don't give a damn what this paper claims; as far as I'm concerned they got these results mixed up with somebody else's," British told herself. She didn't have any regrets about sneaking behind Rue's back and getting a

paternity test or keeping Tia in check. Only regret she had was pretending like she was going to be able to accept Rue's baby. Even if somebody gave British a million dollars she was still not accepting Rue's baby. As far as she was concerned, her and Rue needed to speak immediately about their relationship because whether that was his child or not she still didn't want Rue dealing with Tia or their baby. Somebody was going to have to say goodbye and British was ready to swallow whoever that person had to be.

Since it wasn't no telling when Rue was going to finally come home, British decided she would go back to Tia's house and share the news. British took her usual route to Tia's house like it was just any other day and she was spying on Rue only this day was eerie. When British reached the forefront she saw yellow caution tape everywhere.

"What the fuck happened here?" British said to herself stopping her car in a halt debating if she should even get out of the car so British just pulled to the side and called Rue's phone, but it was going straight to voicemail as usual. British was determined to find out what was going on so she left a message.

"I'm at your baby mother's house and its yellow tape everywhere. I don't know where you at, but you need to get your narrow ass over here now and figure out what the fuck is going on?" If only she knew Rue had already been there and done that.

"I'm goin talk to one of her neighbors and see if they tell me something." British was parked across the street from Tia's house where a lady was sitting on the porch so she got out her car to get some answers.

"Excuse ma'am do you know why all this yellow tape is around Tia's house? Tia and I had plans for today."

"I think that girl done killed that baby; I could've been told y'all that girl was crazy. The police done took her ass away. This block ain't never going to see her again"

British was bamboozled as to why Tia would kill her baby. If she was going to kill anybody she should've killed herself, but British was overjoyed. Now Tia and Rhys were both past-tense variables and Rue could finally focus on having a family and a life with her and only her. As for Tia, karma is a bitch; you should've kept your legs closed bitch and saved yourself an indictment.

$

Feeling like she was in a cell, Passive wanted some medical relief. How about a second opinion from another doctor because this hospital imprisonment shit was starting to become nerve wrecking. You can't make money or run missions sitting and laying on your ass. If only Passive and Smoke would've shut her hospital floor down, maybe Passive would've been safer. No one else besides her visitors should've been allowed on her floor. No one should've been allowed to visit Passive without Smoke's consent or his presence. Currently, she needed just as much protection as the President of the United States. Rock was hired to be her current bodyguard, but he must've turned down the job because he hadn't been guarding Passive since she had been hospitalized. Next in line was Smoke, her husband, whose job was to provide and protect, but he seemed to be off-duty also. There shouldn't have been any off-guard moment in Passive's hospital vacation, but I guess everyone needs a break sometimes.

Passive was just waking up from one of those second trimester naps when she became motionless.

"It's been so long Passive since our last encounter. I see your resting good so your taking care of yourself and the baby well." Cahill determined.

"Why are you here?" At the sight of him Passive wanted to yank the IV out of her arm and strangulate Cahill with it or rip her IV post from its post and make him drown from IV fluids. Either way it goes she wanted to kill him on GP especially after Rock confirming to her that he killed her parents. Every time she looked at him that was all she could see and envision was Cahill killing her parents like she killed Lindsay's mom.

"Is that how you speak to your godfather after all these years?"

"It took me to be hospitalized to get a visit from you, but you consider yourself to be my godparent. As far as I'm concerned my husband is concerned and my child is concerned my godfather is dead to me. I didn't need you then and we don't need you know so you can go back to whatever rock you crawled out of. "

"I'm in awe of your taste in men. You had strong male role models and you choose to settle for a dirty cop? A man who got you slanging drugs for him? You goin throw shade to me and try to tell me your husband can protect you better than I can? How y'all goin get money now that your ass knocked up?"

"Don't worry about me, my life, or my husband. The only strong role model I had was my father until you took him away from me now leave!"

"I have a lot of unfinished business with you but, I have to change my plans since your pregnant now. I don't kill babies especially not unborn babies. I bet you will wear your pregnancy well. I remember when your mother was pregnant with you. She was like 36 weeks pregnant and didn't even look it."

"Don't you ever speak on my father or mother again. I want you to leave!"

"If I leave here your next few visitors might not be so kind to let you live."

"Lindsay cannot kill me she already tried that and failed. You must be considering her to be more than one person."

"She wasn't trying to kill you the first time. I protected you, but this time is different. Newsflash, Lindsay is not the only enemy you got."

"So your going to allow these women to kill me and my baby is that what your telling me?"

"No one is going to touch you or the baby not under my watch. See you next time."

When Cahill left the room, it was like Passive's air waves were blocked. She was just face to face with a man she wanted to murder who now knew she was bearing a child. He also knew about the street beefs she has accumulated being married to Smoke and living her mighty lifestyle. It was like he knew everything that has been transpiring in her life. How in the hell did he know so much?

Now that I'm hospital bound everybody wants to come visit me. As far as I'm concerned who's ever in charge of visitation can permanently terminate and freeze all my visits. I need to make a personalized visitor's list because I see anybody can visit me even shady fucking mayors who claim to be my godfather.

Where the fuck was my godfather when my ass got kidnapped in Missouri? Where the fuck was my godfather when gay bitches was tryna fuck me and stalking me in Kentucky? Where in the fuck was my godfather when Smoke got kidnapped by Lindsay? What type of godfather murders his god child's parents? Fuck a godparent; it was nothing that a godparent could do for me in this lifetime and how in the hell does Cahill know about every little detail that's going on in my life like he has been tracking my routes and lifestyle since my father died. Who in the fuck was his eyes and ears because somebody had to be snitching on me or he is just paying a spy real fucking good. Whatever the case may be I want out of this hospital now. Somebody better help me bust up out of here or I'm going to bust myself up out here my got damn self.

Chapter 11: De Trop

What is worst? Having cobwebs on your coochi from lack of sex or having an effaced coochi from a vicious act of humanity. Paradise was in a whirlwind of karma and spite that almost costed her center counsel. She rather had been lying in the hospital with black eyes, busted lips, or a broken nose then having a grilled cooch. Cahill just couldn't give her a common punishment; he had to inflict something out the norm of normal inflictions.

I don't know what could possibly possess a man to commit such a heinous crime, but you can never underestimate a world with heinous people. Paradise's vagina just received the worst karma ever as it practically melted to the white meat. Rock was right by her bedside and if it wasn't for him more damage would've been done to her internal organs and her internal self.

Paradise had first and second degree burns resulting in blisters, minor inflammation, redness, and thickening of the skin along her hoo-ha. Just think how close Paradise was to third and fourth degree burns. Whatever attempt Cahill was making to eliminate Paradise's vulva from a man's world failed. Doctors said that they would give Paradise's skin a month to heal and if it didn't then the next step would be to perform a medical procedure called skin grafting where you transplant a layer of skin from the body to another part of the body. Paradise was going to need lots of skin care and bandaging, but she was willing to do whatever she had to do to get the appearance of her cunt back to normal. Obviously, Cahill didn't plan on setting eyes or hands on Paradise ever again so that was the least of her worries.

"How you holding up ma?" Rock asked out of major concern.

"I'm in a very awkward place, but I'm glad your here with me now, and I'm glad you rescued me from that monster."

"Have you know that you ain't never going back there. That was his ending now it's my beginning."

"I know I'm glad it's over, but what about Passive? You were supposed to be guarding her right?"

"Once I tell them what happened she'll have compassion."

"Yea right she'll probably laugh at me."

"I cleared your name with Passive so ain't no smoke there. I refused to give up Cahill until I had her word on your safety."

"I'm just in awe like I've really been doing some terrible things to people and I feel like I deserve this. This is a wake-up call for me to get my shit together because my losses have changed. I actually have things that I can lose right now and I don't want to lose anymore. I want to win with you and everyone else who is willing to put the old Paradise behind them."

"Don't worry I'll never let you lose," Rock kissed Paradise on the forehead.

"Okay please go inform Passive you are okay because I don't want you to have no problems with any of them. We got enough problems on our plate as is."

"I'll be back then baby I'm just goin run to the waiting area, stare out the huge hospital windows, and fill her in on the details. I'm just goin put my security job on hold until you are freed from these hospital limits. You shouldn't be here longer than a few more days."

"I hope not because I hate hospitals, hospital food, the smell of hospitals, fake ass caring hospital nurses just everything."

When Rock hit the hallway, his thirst started quenching so he decided to hit the cafeteria for a fountain drink. Soon as the elevator opened he saw a familiar face. Rock hoped that this time they could talk like grown men, but that was a misconception. Rock and Smoke started tussling like it was a boxing championship.

"I didn't even want you around but Passive did. I can't believe I trusted you to look after her." Smoke snuck in breathing heavily.

"Listen, Cahill set Paradise's juice box afire: I've been here at the hospital with her iust like you've been at your woman's bedside I've been at mines. I was coming back on duty soon as she was released. I was just about to call y'all and let y'all know."

The whole time they were wrestling the elevator was just wandering aimlessly up and down its course. Its doors would open and close and nobody dared to enter and disturb them or snitch on them. Switching leads from Smoke to Rock they finally roughed each other up enough and took a breather. The two of them just sat down in the elevator against the elevator's corners on chill mode.

"I'm sick of hearing about this Cahill nigga. He's like a cancer just like Lindsay I swear them two must be related."

"They might be in cahoots with each other."

"Clearly we fighting the wrong people and we need to get on the sane page because we need to dispose of these two bastards constantly protruding in our lives."

"I can agree to that," Rock and Smoke made a decisive pact to ride on their enemies in the name of love. It was time all past beef was thrown aside and they joined forces. One man can change the world, but two men could change the universe.

$

With nothing, but sunny days in the weekly forecast Rue migrated to Nevada. It's been a few calendars since he's seen his dad so he decided to pay him a visit, release some tension, and get a man's point of view on the issues he's been dealing with.

At High Desert State Prison, Rue visited his father Zay.

"What's up pops, how you been living?"

"I've been good it's about time you brought your scrawny ass up here to visit me."

"I just been dealing with a lot and decided to take a road trip up here and make sure your still alive."

"The gesture is appreciated, but I know you. It's some deep shit going on in your life and you came up here to share. It's nothing like a father's comfort when a woman breaks the spirit of comfort."

"Before I go off into my story, why don't you tell me what's been shaking in your personal life?"

"Well I have a good woman by my side, her name is Andrea and we have a very strong relationship even though I'm behind bars. She always tells me stories about her kids and most of them are about her son Smoke, her daughter Omani, or her daughter-in-law Passive. I would love for y'all to meet each other one day. She's now the guardian of my daughter Zana and I love her more than I've ever loved any women."

"I'm glad you finally got a good woman; I can't seem to get away from all the floozies. My girlfriend British is a selfish-ungrateful bitch, but she has done a lot of shit for me and I love her. Then it's my baby mother Tia who just murdered your first grandchild and my first son. How in the fuck am I supposed to live with myself with that void? It's a hole in my heart now like an Atrial Septal Defect; I can't eat, I can't sleep, and I can't think and to be honest I don't even know if the baby was actually mine or not. My girlfriend hated Tia and begged me to stay away from her. In some twisted way she was right. I understand I hurt her by this so I feel like I should just let her go and let her find somebody who can love her correctly."

"Damn son that's fucked up that's life for you."

"I want to kill her for what she did to that baby; I want to go to whatever cell she's at or psych ward and off her ass the same way she killed that baby."

"Look at me son; this is not the life you want."

"If you want to kill her so bad, why don't you get somebody else to do it, make somebody else take the fall. You say you got a down ass bitch by your side so I'm sure if you put all the love you put into that baby into her you can persuade her to do anything."

"You right pops, I'm sure she would kill that bitch for me like I said she hates her."

"Cheer the fuck up and get yourself back in the game. Don't let these hoes keep you down. It does seem to me like British is the one you should've been loving solely all this time. You have got to admit you set yourself up for this shit by being lustful, but it's not too late to make things right it's never too late for that."

"Well, it's been good seeing you and talking to you pops. You stay up."

"Likewise, you know where I'm at so don't be no stranger and remember what I said. Next time you come I would like for you to meet my family."

"Anything for your pop, bet that up."

Now with Rue's fathers help he was more level-headed and ready to touch down in Detroit and apologize to British for all of his recent bullshit. This couldn't be no basic apology either because British wasn't trying to hear just a plain "I'm sorry." Gifts really set an apology off especially when the gift represented something long-term. Him and British had been through a world war of shit and he wanted to spend each and every day with her for the rest of his life. Soon as he reached Michigan soil, Rue was going straight to a jewelry store to buy British an engagement ring. As far as everything with Tia he could discuss her nothingness future after he prepared for

British's special bombshell.

Chapter 12: Solitary Dispatch

Doctors finally were going to release their most peculiar patient ever in their hospital history. Continuously forced to use female anatomy vocabulary without being unprofessional was a challenge to both the men and women doctors who encountered Paradise because of her condition. Someone set her vagina on fire, how else do you identify her besides labeling her as the girl with the burnt vagina or flaming vagina, or something to that extent. The only time the ER really had to deal with coochi patients was mainly in case of pregnancy or STD.

When Rock came back to Paradise's room, she had good news and she hoped that Rock's talk with Passive went smoothly and he would have good news as well.

"The doctors said I can leave as soon as I sign my release papers so can you hand me that black ink pen over there."

"Your kidding right."

"I'm not kidding; I'm free to go. You can go ask the doctors if you don't believe me."

"No, I believe you; we've been praying for this day."

"And now that this day is finally here what are we going to do? Where are we going to go?"

"We're still going to go out of state, but before we leave I got one last thing to take care of."

"I bet it has something to do with Passive right? I knew she wasn't going to just spare my life. I told you she wasn't now what are we going to do?"

"Just calm down baby; Smoke and I are going to join forces and we're going to take out Cahill together and Lindsay as well so can you stay put for me until then? The game has changed with Passive she's pregnant right now she is not in the condition to smoke anybody."

"I trust you Rock just go holler at Smoke and see what's next for us," Rock kissed Paradise.

$

It was very uncommon for Passive to have a public announcement involving the people that were closest to her, but this time was different. Baby Passive was in jeopardy beyond medical jeopardy and Passive had to protect her baby. There was no way in hell she could be pregnant and incarcerated. Something had to be done ASAP so Passive called Smoke and he answered his phone on the 1st ring as always.

"Everything okay Passive?"

"I know you probably hate my guts still, but we are beyond that. I need you, Elvia, and Posh to come down to the hospital right now, I won't talk to anyone about what is going on unless all of you are present. Are you following me?"

"I got you."

Smoke feeling extra curious did exactly as he was instructed. Hopefully, Posh was going to be in town because she was always on the move from state to state with Corbin. Every since Passive had been in the hospital Posh had been making sure she stayed in Michigan or near Michigan in case of emergency.

Mostly, Smoke wondered what had manifested so fast to cause the extra two party meeting. All Passive should've needed was Smoke, but he guessed this is what happens when a woman gets sisters by life. They always have to be included in everything, but nobody should be included in marital decisions. As far as Smoke was concerned anything that concerned her safety and well-being and this baby was a marital matter.

Just like Passive said the three people she requested arrived in her room pronto at the same time. Smoke being the gentleman that he was, was the last one to enter because he let the ladies go first.

"I'm glad you all came."

"Let's do an ice breaker now. I'm just kidding," Elvia spoofed.

"Why have you brought us all together?" Posh spoke up and out first.

"I had a visit from Cahill; I can no longer stay in this hospital. Y'all better selectively come up with a plan that doesn't include me being here or else I will take matters into my own hands."

"Here you go again being secretive. I need to know shit like this the very second it happens," Smoke grilled Passive.

"The very second it happened I could barely even move. I'm surprise I was even able to talk. I was on the verge of killing him then and there, but I knew this hospital wasn't the time or place."

"Why do you need Elvia and Posh here for this determination?"

"You can't be around me 24/7 but, they can. You requested Rock's service so where the fuck was he at when public enemy#1 came strolling in my room playing god daddy?"

"Rock was here, he just wasn't directly in here with you. He has some private issues that he is dealing with right now, but we have agreed to resolve our issues for the greater good of our families. In the meantime, I can't quit my job to be your personal servant for 24 hours a day."

"You guys don't need to fight right now everybody be cool." Elvia attempted to make rational peace.

"What's got into you Smoke that was so rude of you," Passive frowned.

"You and Elvia's little stunt with Gab has come back to bite us in the ass. Gab has kidnapped Omani and Onyx, Grant might be dead now, and ain't no telling what else he has done or is going to do. I want to rescue her but, I can't leave you alone with anybody at any second. We got people waiting on me to drop the ball so they can harm you. I can't let anything happen to you or our baby."

"I'm sorry Smoke; I should've known something was wrong other than our current situation."

"I'm sorry too this is my sister we talking about. She's done a lot in the past, but it ain't no telling what Gab is going to do to her."

"That's why y'all need to get me out of this hospital before the Monarchs come find me here and "who knows who else.""

"Your right Passive, we're just going to have to get you a house doctor."

"I wish y'all would've been done that, but we don't have time to argue and reflect on the past. We got to worry about the present and the future. Elvia, I need you to go get me a change of clothes, a wig, a gun and some sunglasses.

"Hold it, hold it, just hold it! Passive you getting ahead of yourself; you don't need a gun when you got us," Smoke declared.

"I do need a gun so don't try to tell me what I do and don't need. Continuing on Posh you and Corbin leave the truck open so we can just hop in it and find me and Smoke another one of low-key house and be back here in 30 minutes. Everybody please be on time because if I stay here any longer I'm going to gag. All hospitals make me sick from the smell of them, to the way they look, and the way they smell. The women walk out with the women, and the men walk out with the men. I think long as we hit the stairways, we'll be out of sight. By the time a nurse realizes I'm gone I'll be miles and miles away."

Entering Passive's room, Rock wasn't trying to intrude on anything, but what he had to say needed immediate attention.

"I'm sorry to barge in on y'all like this."

"What's going on Rock?" Both Passive and Smoke questioned Rock in the same breath.

"The hospital is releasing Paradise and I was wondering if y'all had somewhere I can take her."

"Sorry Rock, but we're breaking Passive up out of here; it's too dangerous for her to be here. Cahill visited her and if he knows she's here and why she's here it's no telling who else knows."

"Cahill? I really got to get Paradise out of here then. He just set her pussy on fire and he has done plenty crude things to her in the past. It's no telling what his next move is going to be please, take Paradise with you guys, and let's go handle Cahill like we said. We need to handle this nigga now; I'm not taking no more chances."

Is Rock out of his fucking mind? Just because I agreed to let the bitch be doesn't means I want the bitch anywhere near me. I forgive her, but I didn't forget, and I'm not going to forget what she did. I don't give a fuck about what pact Rock and Smoke made. Smoke can kill

Cahill by his got damn self if it's like that.

"You stepping out of bounds with that request Rock," Passive determined.

"Passive, don't be cold-hearted about this; Cahill is a canker just like Lindsay and if we don't stop them now they're going to keep being a threat to us and keep hurting people. Is that what you want? I'm not asking you to be Paradise's best friend or even speak to her just let her come with y'all until I come back to get her."

"Okay, but if that bitch even looks at me shady, I'm killing her."

"You don't have to worry about no grims or no grimaces; I promise you that," Rock left out the room to get Paradise.

Snapping back into action Passive continued in her break-out rant; somebody better Google how to take out an IV because this IV gotta go. I guess I see why people say hospitals kill people; you just never know until you are in one and you actually witness what goes on.

Everybody came back in 30 minutes ready to furtively evacuate Passive from the premises. Rock returned to the room with Paradise who were both quiet as a church mouse. Elvia brought Passive a cute little velour jogging suit, fresh panties, with a pink wig so Passive went to the bathroom and attempted to change her clothes when she realized that she should probably get her IV taken out first before she covers it up with her clothing.

"So who's going to take out my IV?"

"I'll do it baby, I think I have the most training to handle IV's," Smoke claimed so he took the tape off of Passive's IV, removed the needle out, threw the needle away, and used a cotton ball to put pressure on the IV spot to make sure it wouldn't bleed. Everyone including Passive was impressed by her man's medical skills.

"Didn't know you had it in you baby."

"You'll be surprised what I'm capable of. That didn't hurt did it?"

"Nope, I didn't feel a thing." After that Passive changed her clothes, put on her wig, put her sunglasses on, and put her gun in her purse.

"Let's go guys, Paradise you exit with us and Rock you exit with Smoke." Just like that Passive, Posh, Paradise, and Elvia exited the hospital with nobody stopping them and after they exited Smoke, Rock, and Corbin was coming right behind them with no problems either.

"I hope you ready for this road trip Passive," Posh stated once everybody was seated in the truck.

"I'm far from ready, but I have no choice, but to make it do what it do. We're going to have to make more stops then in any road trip I've ever taken. Maybe I can just sleep through this whole road trip thing, but somehow, someway I bet this baby is going to find a way to wake me up."

"Just focus on you and the baby Passive and let us do the rest."

Chapter 13: Solidified

The most rewarding part of anger is having the ability to maximize your anger through somebody else. Since Lindsay put British in charge of her vendettas, it was time to strike. British was heated; she hadn't seen or heard from Rue in what seemed like forever. She didn't have a link or trace to him like a cold case so as far as she was concerned he could French kiss her ass. British wasn't the one that killed your baby apparently that bitch was in jail, but since home wasn't home no more and Rue was treating British sour over another bitch's mistakes he could be cut off as well.

Prime time for her to live up to her last name Chambers' and put somebody in a chamber. Who was going to be her second victim since she had already succeeded in kidnapping a newborn baby? Why not Kyra? She was the eldest sister of Smoke and a sister who had never succumbed to any of her big brother's enemies' backlash. Now that she was in charge nobody was exempt or untouchable.

Kyra's inhabitance was in Missouri; British was no longer in the driving mood. Best thing to do was to walk away from a crime rather than flee from a crime in a vehicle. British had never ridden a train before, but always wanted to so Amtrack it was. The shortest train from the D to Kansas City was 5 hours and 29 minutes. A roundtrip ticket was going to run between 100 and 300 bucks, but it was definitely going to be money well spent. Money was like a windfall anyway with Lindsay throwing out cheddar for British and her mischief.

According to her findings, British found out that Kyra's exact location was Kansas City, Missouri. It was a geographical fact that it was the largest city in the state of Missouri; but wasn't nothing geographically challenging to British though, especially not terrorizing another Mitchell. Kyra was living with good company too; she had a fiancé named Cos who she was actively planning a spring wedding with according to social media, but none of that mattered.

When British reached Kansas City she checked in a hotel, arranged an UBER, and took it to Kyra's residence. Her UBER driver was a black woman who was very affable and seemed like she would be down for the cause so British didn't hesitate to get to know her driver.

"Look Cabbie, you've been driving me around for a couple of rides so why not keep this relationship going because I need a personal driver for the duration of my time here in Missouri."

"My name is Sosina people call me Sina, let's just cut straight to the chase. How much money we talking and what type of driving do you want because it looks like you want a getaway driver? I just got off probation man I hope you know what you doing why you got me riding you around participating in your hot shit."

"I can't tell you what my plan is; I just need you to have my back when I say it's time to go. I don't need no questions or no extra drama you just do as I say, and I'll give you the best cab tip you'll probably ever receive in your life."

"I'm in because you look like a bag of money."

For a couple of days, British just made observations so she could brainstorm exactly how she was going to catch Kyra slipping. Kyra didn't have no regular routine except at 9:00AM every morning she went jogging around her complex. Joggers are always getting caught up in somebody's crime, and that's why people should get a gym membership or buy some fitness equipment for your house. Three days after British coming into town, her and her usual driver Sina from day one followed Kyra to a bar. The killing part about everything was how her plan was working itself out naturally. Kyra came out the bar staggering drunk, saw the cab, and just opened the back door to the cab and got in.

"I need a ride please take me home," Kyra claimed with alcoholic funk reeking from her breath. Kyra didn't even notice British sitting in the back seat of the cab along with her like she had tunnel vision.

"Where do you live?"

"I stay, I stay fifteen minutes from here on Clover," Kyra couldn't even get her words out before she opened up the cab door and vomited.

"I'm sorry I just had a miscarriage. I just don't know what to do with my life anymore. I don't know who made miscarriages and why did I have to have one," Kyra confessed. British just kept her cool and played along with Sina like she wasn't there. After Kyra vomited some more and let the cab take off, a few seconds later she passed out in the backseat like she was home in her own bed.

Drunk sleep was the best sleep in the world, it wasn't about to be no waking up Kyra which was perfectly fine because British had other motives for her.

"This is crazy how this broad just fell into our laps; you remember what I was telling you about Sina. This is the time; I need you to drive like you in a stoly and make your way to Longview Lake. We're about to leave this dumb broad stranded in the middle of a lake."

"I would hate to be that bitch she just had a miscarriage and now your about to leave her floating on a lake? What the fuck did she do to you?"

"Her family and my family are at war and I'm just exercising the art of war. Killing a bitch is easy, but there are many levels too torturing, and being stuck in the middle of nowhere without a phone, when nobody knows where you at, when you don't know when help is coming, with nothing to eat is a hellified payback better than an easy death."

"Okay, just don't do that shit to me if I ever make you mad remember I'm just the driver and driving is all I do."

"Stay focus."

Upon reaching Longview Lake, Kyra was still laying wildly on the backseat dormant.

"Help me get her out the car," British prompted Sina.

"I thought we agreed I'm just your driver, your compass, your navigator?"

"Look money talks and I got a lot of it; we ain't killing anybody so shut up and help me carry her to the lake." Fuck the money; rich people go to jail all the time. Money ain't shit anyway when your ass in jail and your bank account is frozen. Sina didn't want to carry shit, but a purse, some shoes or something, but she didn't know what British was capable of so she did as she was asked.

"This girl is so petite she must not eat meat," Sina evaluated.

"I don't care what she eats," Sina and British temporary laid Kyra on the ground.

It was a canoe suspended onto the dock; Sina and British looked at the canoe then they looked at each other.

"So what you want me to row too?" Sina asked. As far as Sina was concerned, when she returned home, she was going to quit her taxi job. People who get into taxis are crazier then what they perceive to be, and Sina wasn't down to go for nobody's joy ride again.

"We can take turns if that makes you feel better." Once again British and Sina lifted Kyra up and put her in the canoe then Sina begin rowing to this big, old buoy British kept pointing at.

"What the fuck are we going to do with a body and a buoy?"

"Just wait to we get there and you'll see."

Positioning the canoe directly next to the buoy, British searched for something to use to tie Kyra to it. Inside the canoe was a round of rope so British had Sina hold Kyra upright extending Kyra's arms so she could tie her to the buoy. Once Kyra was tied, Sina and British freed the rest of Kyra's body and let it droop off the buoy and into the water. British rowed back to the dock like she was in a canoe competition before the cold water awakened Kyra.

British wanted to pat herself on the back, but she couldn't have completed this task without Sina. Soon as they hit the dock, they tied the canoe back there and got in the car ready for a debate.

"What are you like 30 years old working a poverty stricken job that you will never be able to advance with? You need to reassess your dull ass life and come run missions with me. My next stop is Kentucky."

"As of right now I'm quitting my job and I'm going to ride out with you until the wheels falls off. We can conquer the world together."

"Yes, now we're getting somewhere."

Chapter 14: Biker Boys

Fifteen minutes into The Monarchs victory of capturing Omani and Onyx, they surmised it was time for the scrutiny to begin. The Monarchs all parked in unison to hurry up and abominate these two predators. Onyx was first to reap the punishment of capture. Two men held Onyx in place so he couldn't break away. One of The Monarchs Lincoln took a rope and tied a loose loop around Onyx's neck like he was about to hang him on a tree and pull the rest of the rope until it's tightest to slowly suffocate him. All Onyx could think about was how and why in the hell him and Omani ended up in this predicament. Clearly, they took their beef with their enemies very seriously because they wasn't about to just wreck some lives; they were about to wipeout lives and more lives until they were satisfied.

"So much for being modern since I see y'all kill people like its 1850 huh?"

"You got some jokes in you now, but let's see will you have some joking in you in a few moments."

Once the rope was set around Onyx's neck, another Monarch (Vallen) strolled up to Onyx after walking past Omani, smacking her on her ass unfriendly, and slobbering over her.

"Have you ever seen a nigga fuck your bitch?" Vallen asked Onyx.

"No, but I have seen another bitch fuck my bitch," Onyx spat back.

Vallen couldn't marble if Onyx was being sarcastic or honest so he hit Onyx with a blow to the stomach that made him cough up blood.

"I'm about to fuck your bitch on my bike right now and let my niggas tag team her ass and my bitch while you sit here and watch."

"She just had a baby; she doesn't need to be engulfing in any sexual activity. If y'all are going to kill us then just kill us, but don't torture her like that."

"Damn you almost convinced me to give two fucks but I don't. You should've said the bitch had AIDS but since she don't she's still fuckable."

It was real nippy outside, but the Monarchs didn't give a shit what the temperature was.

"You got the camera Gab so Smoke can see his little bitty sister get fucked by a gang of niggas. And she can add this sex tape to her collection since she's into that kinky shit. Didn't think I knew that Omani did you?"

"Fuck you and your so called knowledge of me."

"Rip her clothes off y'all all of them. Her words irritate me; I want to hear her scream and cry."

Onyx kept trying to get at each and every Monarch that stood close by him, but he just kept getting hit with blow after blow.

The Monarchs ripped off Omani's clothes until she was completely bare-skinned. They hog tied her wrists to the outposts on the back wheel so she would be facing Onyx, the camera, and everybody else. Her ass was in the air and face was down on the seat cushion like a little horny prostitute. .

The Monarchs cheered at this fine piece of ass they had smack, dab, and in the center of them.

"Whooooooot!" It looked like celebrity pussy the way they had Omani arched up.

Vallen and his girlfriend Vivienne had two, cold Moet bottles and much as Vivienne loved her Moet, she cracked open one bottle and douched it on Omani like a champagne shower.

"Yeah, my nigga like when I clean bitches and guess what you looking real scummy right now you scumbag ass bitch; want to go in the forest and murder people ass bitch; who calling the shots now bitch? Take this shit you deserve everything that's coming to you despicable ass bitch, got my squad on you like a porno ass bitch," Vivienne said as she shook wet champagne all over Omani's body from the top of her head to her feet.

Omani was taken aback by this random bubbly assault because nobody had ever poured anything on her other then syrup or honey. This was not some kinky shit; this was some file, chilly shit and whatever was going to happen next, Omani just wanted them to get it over with. This was not the time to be wasting champagne or degrading bitches when Omani and Onyx had missions to do. *This old rapping ass bitch needs to go take five seats behind this whole motorcycle clan and go find an open mic somewhere why she trying spit bars while she accosts me.*

"You damn right baby show that bitch who the boss," Vallen commented.

Drenched up with champagne still drip dropping down her face and infusing into her pores, Omani needed answers.

"What the fuck is this, an x-rated contest?"

"This is a sex tape and you the star," Cruise answered.

Circling around Omani like a swarm of killer bees was the camera man Cruise. He was zooming and catching shots blooming from every angle like he took classes to be a porno videographer. For a second Cruise turned the camera on himself.

"Look at your little adorable sister Smoke about to get freaked the fuck out. She's our little truffle butter cup now; who's the jack in the box now you old mark ass nigga since you want to send your wifey to fight your battles how does this battle feel? By the way your sister fine as fuck and this tape right here goin make millions. We goin sell this shit to Playboy, playboy," Cruise laughed evilly. The camera was back on Omani now.

"Ram that shit up her ass one time for Smoke." Vivienne spread Omani's butt cheeks, caressed her ass, and did as Cruise commanded and tears crawled from up under Omani's eyelids mixing in with the champagne drops that were still gradually sliding off of her.

"Ram it up her ass again for Passive." Omani compressed her inner strength tightly again enduring the pain and discomfiture. Omani had never let anybody have permission to fuck her in her ass or involuntarily fuck her in the ass. Guess it was a first time for everything.

"Now ram it up her ass again one good time for the Monarchs. Nobody got an ark like a Monarch," Omani clenched up again. Each time Vivienne jammed the bottle up her anus she pushed the whole bottle inside of Omani's ass until you could see the bottom of the bottle in between her cheeks.

"Relax for a second Omani baby, but were not done with you yet so don't get happy." Omani felt perishable; after this blatant niggerdom she didn't even want to think twice about sex.

Now it was Vallen's turn and he took Vivienne's bottle and pushed it and pulled it from wall to wall and depth to depth until Omani screamed a piercing orgasm.

"Nooooo! Please stop!"

"You said keep going?"

"I said stop!"

"Where your smart ass mouth at now?" Omani felt like her internal organs were punctured and breaking off into fragmentations inside of her stomach.

"You want me to stop, but you got some female excretions seeping out so you must like this shit."

"I don't like this; y'all have done enough. Why aren't y'all doing this to Passive instead of me and Smoke? They the ones you really want."

"Cut the camera off Cruise and forward that shit to Smoke," Gab ordered.

"Actually no, scratch that shit, I got a better idea," Gab pulled Cruise off to the side so nobody, but Cruise could hear him.

"In the morning we're going to drop this tape off at UPS and send that shit to the 11th Precinct same day delivery so everybody at Smoke's job can watch his little sister get sodomized. We're going to send that shit to the evidence department. The police are bound to watch an evidence tape quick especially if we call them and give them an anonymous tip about an evidence tape coming from Missouri."

"Gab, are your balls really that big? This is a police station we're talking about; ain't none of us have any masks, and the fact that this is Smoke's precinct I'm sure they will find a way to prosecute us to the fullest extent."

"We can stay here; we don't have to go back to Michigan. We can change our motorcycle name and use a bogus address for UPS so nothing comes back to us. Smoke might know who we are, but he doesn't know where we are. He might run shit in Michigan, but he don't run shit here."

"You sound fucking selfish! I think you've taken this thing to fucking far."

"If you don't like what I'm doing you can leave, but let's not forget who was filming all this shit. You picked the wrong time to choose a stance; I can turn this whole motorcycle group against you and kill you so get with the program. Go think about some new motorcycle names while I finish talking to this lousy bitch."

"Back to you sweet-tart; if you want a reaction out of somebody you don't go after them head-up, you go after they family first so they'll know you mean business."

"I'm somebody's mother and y'all just sodomized me twice with a bottle."

"Keep talking shit and we'll do it again, but since your somebody's momma you can stay in the au naturel and chained up on somebody's bike like your somebody's bitch, and your boo boo can continue to watch over you. You better hope nobody else catches your asshole or your pussy hole slipping."

Just like that, the Monarchs disappeared into an abandoned clubhouse and left their prisoners and their bikes ducked off on a foreign farmland ready to camp out for the night.

Chapter 15: The Crazy Horse

If Charlotte had a web, maybe she wouldn't be so unbalanced. She presumed Lindsay was going to sick all her contracted goons on her, but first Lindsay would have to find her. Plus nobody was going to kill Charlotte first; killing Charlotte would be second after Amory was rescued. If Charlotte made it that far because you'll be surprised what sharp shooting snipers could do.

Coasting prudently, Charlotte couldn't make-up her mind on what she should do with Amory. It was between returning her to her rightful owners or selling her. Amory had the potential to be a down payment for Charlotte's new lifestyle, and she knew just the right people. Selling babies was a division in the black market world that was slapping because there were copious types of women scavenging for a baby. Women paid bands for multiple natures of fertilizations, fertility interventions, and just top dollar moncy to have the best of the best fertility specialists just to conceive. Why pay bands for that when you could hit the black market and just buy a baby? Mad scientists were cloning babies, adopting babies, and selling babies to oversea markets. Wouldn't you rather see a baby in a woman's arms being loved and nurtured then in a back alley trashcan or river bend dead and mutilated?

In no way did Charlotte want harm to come to Amory. She just wanted to ditch the kid for some money so she could get the hell out of dodge before Lindsay got whiff of her. If Passive thought she mutilated Liz Chambers, she was wrong because Lindsay was going to butcher Charlotte's body for kidnapping her mental daughter/niece, and Charlotte knew it because she was warned. Amory was going to be waking up soon needing a feeding and a changing, so Charlotte had to operate swiftly. The clock was tick-tocking hour after hour, minute after minute, and second after second.

In this game, it was about who you know because what you know didn't really count for shit. Since, Charlotte knew a key game player in the black market; she decided to give him a buzz.

"Hello, this is Cahill."

"How much is a newborn baby girl retailing for in that murky network of yours?"

"Don't ask me direct questions like that before you announce yourself to me. Who am I speaking with?"

"This is Charlotte; the only blood cousin you know named Charlotte. Charlotte, who you devised me to work with egghead ass Lindsay Chambers, Charlotte."

"My bad I haven't spoken with you since you've been at her leisure. How exactly is that going for you? Is Lindsay a great employer or what?"

"Cut the shit Cahill, I can't believe you got me in this mishmash. You told me this bitch was shady, but you never said that she be kidnapping babies, and I was going to be somebody's babysitter. This shit is played out and I want out and your going to pay for all of my time you let your brainsick friend waste."

"What are you talking about?"

"You told that trick to put me on and she put me on as the babysitter of a baby she had to have kidnapped because I know for a fact she cannot possibly have any kids' right? Ain't no man desperate enough to willingly pop a nut up in her."

"I'm not goin lie she never had a child since I've known her and I've been knowing her for a long minute and working with her very closely."

"Screw all of that, Lindsay was trying to kill me so I fled the house in the quickness and I took the baby with me so can you help me flip this baby or nah? You the one that got me in this mayhem now get me out of it." Cahill thought to himself briefly. He knew Omani's baby was missing because he knew anything and everything that involved Passive and her Mitchell family tree so Lindsay must've kidnapped Omani's baby and that must be the baby that Charlotte had. Little did Charlotte know exactly how much Omani's baby meant to him.

"Yeah, I can how much you want for her?"

"I want at least 50,000 racks." Cahill was geeked all he had to cough up was 50 g's because he was banking on coughing up 100 g's or more for such a prize possession. Charlotte just cheated herself out of a heap of money, but you get what you ask for just like you get what you pay for.

"No problem, I got you, but listen to me and listen to me carefully."

"Wait, why does it sound like you are buying this baby from me? What is your interest in this whole ordeal?"

"That baby that you have is my daughter and nobody knows that except me, Omani the mother, and now you. I just got into some shady shit myself and I want to relocate out of the country for good and I want to take my daughter with me. I want to turn over a new leaf with her and just put my shady reputation behind me. Don't even think about suggesting me and her mother come to a collective agreement because her mother didn't even tell me my child was born. She had that nigga all up in the hospital playing daddy to my daughter we created like I'm some type of deadbeat or something."

"Okay just tell me when and where and I'm there."

"I've been driving for hours and remember passing signs that said I was entering Minnesota. When I feel like Amory and I are safe, I will situate somewhere and let you know where my destination is."

"Okay, but you can't tell anybody what I've told you about Amory being my daughter. You can't communicate with anybody on the telephone, and you got to stay away from people and public places because you never know what or when your going to pop up on a news channel. Please take care of my daughter for me; I've never even seen her before or held her and I don't want nothing to go wrong."

"I got you I want jeopardize this it's a lot at stake here."

Baby Amory was exposing the sensitive side of Cahill and the more he contemplated on why Lindsay decided to kidnap Omani's baby the more caustic he became. *I know that bitch didn't think I was just goin toot it and boot it one time. Granted, I didn't expect to have a baby with her, and we made a verbal agreement that I would let Omani raise the baby with her man just so nobody in my life or her life would have to suffer from our affairs. As far as Lindsay, I'm stunned she would involve a baby in her beef with Passive and Smoke unless Omani was now added to that beef, but kidnapping a newborn baby was pretty declass for somebody as canny as Lindsay. If it was any other person's baby I probably wouldn't give a damn, but this was my baby who Lindsay kidnapped.*

Granted, if Amory wasn't kidnapped and Charlotte didn't proposition me, I wouldn't be able to take custody of her as fast as I am. I was goin get my baby regardless of any ruse I had to use.

Besides, I don't know what gave Lindsay the idea to think she was going to kill one of mines.

Lindsay had no idea that Charlotte and Cahill were related or that Cahill was using Charlotte as his insider. He felt obscure that out of all the jobs Lindsay could give somebody, she made Charlotte be a nanny.

Although, Lindsay may not be one to tell somebody her every move; when she moved, she just moved, and this was the wrong move for her. She should've kept her evil claws off of Amory Mitchell whose name should've been Amory Caesar. Soon as me and Amory go over a couple of borders and settle into our place, I'm goin body that bitch along with our so called partnership.

Chapter 16: Crazed Cooling

All was going swell with Lindsay and her wicked pregnancy. This was the least shadiest time out of her whole entire life. Lindsay was one month ahead of Passive and was letting British get down and dirty while she just laid back and masked in pregnant virtues. Couldn't nothing possibly rain on her charades, not even the possibility that her so called alliances were being broken and waiting to retaliate against her and her enemies who she thought she outsmarted were gaining on her.

Departing from the others, Elvia, Posh, and Paradise let Passive, Smoke, and Corbin make their way to Indiana so they could finish their business in Michigan. Wasn't no sense in super back-trailing when they were already in Michigan.

"Paradise, you have to go with us," Elvia and Posh ordered her.

"I need to sit down and heal."

"Listen, you don't deserve to be here right now under our security. We're not going to leave you alone with Passive so it's not a choice. When we come back to join Passive you can come back to rejoin Passive, and hopefully by then Rock will be back."

Rock jumped off their band wagon too planning to post up in Michigan until Smoke could accompany him.

Finally in Marquette, Michigan, Elvia and Posh had two addresses to work with and a gallery of pictures of Lindsay. They figured they would check out the houses first then canvass those neighborhoods. Neighbors were nosey as hell and they knew everything; somebody was bound to have loose lips.

At house number one, Posh and Elvia surveyed the area and saw a man enter the house through the front door who appeared to be a single man. All the lights were off when he entered the house which meant it wasn't anybody there to turn them on or off other than him.

"I guess a man lives here now," Posh stated.

"That doesn't mean we're going to just leave here without asking any questions."

"So what approach should we take? Should we kick the door down, break in, or just force our way in?"

"I'm goin knock on the door and you goin come from the side of the house with your gun and point it at his stomach and then we'll just go from there."

"Bet let's get it." Out of nowhere Posh pulled some handcuffs out her purse and handcuffed Paradise's wrists to the automatic shift gear. Distinctly, Paradise stuck her wrists out to be handcuffed without hassle.

"What type of kinky shit you be on Posh carrying handcuffs in your purse? What you got sex toys in their too?"

"Don't ask questions about my sex life. Trust me you don't want to know the answer to those."

"Your right let's change the subject. You better sit tight and sit quiet in here while we go take care of this business. Are we clear Paradise?"

"We're clear I will not move,"

Getting out the car, Elvia went to the door and rung the doorbell and stood on the porch like she was trying to advertise something.

"How can I help you?" The man opened his door.

"You can help me by telling me where the fuck Lindsay Chambers is?" As Elvia was talking, Posh came from the side of the house with her gun and pressed it on the man's side like she was about to iron his stomach with it.

"Is this really necessary for you gals to be pulling out your weapons and things and pointing them at me?" Elvia pushed the man into Lindsay's house with their guns and closed the front door behind them.

"Keep your hands up where we can see them while we're talking to you. All this is necessary because we believe your hiding a criminal in your home."

"I got my hands up geez why do y'all have to be so violent with me? We can talk about whatever you want to talk about minus the guns and the violence."

"No Simon we can't," Elvia read off of the guy's mechanic jacket.

"I'm goin ask you one time and one time only so you better answer right. Where the fuck is Lindsay Chambers?"

"I don't know anybody who goes by that name ladies. I swear I'm telling y'all the truth."

"Wrong answer Simon? Take your ass up the stairs to that nice ass balcony you got."

"Why do we have to switch rooms I thought we was having a good, old conversation in the open right where we were?"

Posh hit Simon in the head with her gun a couple of times while he was leading them to the balcony. Once outside on the balcony Elvia yelled, "now turn around and look down." Elvia ran up behind him and held his head over the balcony.

"A woman name Lindsay Chambers owns this house now either you tell me where I can find her or you give me her number."

"I told you I don't know any Lindsay Chambers and don't no Lindsay Chambers own this house. Why won't y'all believe me?"

"We have a lease that says Lindsay Chambers owns this house so clearly if your here she subleased this house to you. I liked you Simon, but your time is up," Elvia pushed Simon off of his tall, balcony causing him to snap his neck when he hit the concrete in his backyard. Wasn't going to be no resuscitating him- he was dead. Quizzically,

Elvia and Posh just looked at each other and left to go to House #2.

$

Charlotte landed in Virginia, Minnesota in Saint Louis County alongside the Mesabi Iron Range. The state had an atmosphere that was so refreshing, Charlotte was thinking about the city and state being her official inhabitance. She could see herself starting all over here with the reputation of being the Queen City of the North she couldn't go wrong. In the middle of the city was a 110 inch 10 legged water tower painted white and baby blue and was one of the cities greatest landmarks. Charlotte figured this would be a great landmark for her and Cahill to meet up.

Gazing outside her hotel room, Charlotte had front rows seats to the beautiful water tower.

"How would you like to meet your daddy today? No more of that brain-dead ass woman. I know she took you from somebody else, I promise you will never have to go back there. Your daddy is coming to get you today," Charlotte played with Amory making her giggle.

It was time to make the call to Cahill before anymore time passed by so everybody can move on with their lives.

"Hey, Cahill what's going on?"

"I'm ready to make this trip to you where you at?"

"I'm in Virginia, Minnesota, how long is it going to take you to get here?"

"I'm going to catch a plane there so I shouldn't be longer than a few hours. Kiss my baby for me okay. Tell her daddy is on his way."

"You got it captain I already told her that, but I will reiterate it."

Every since Cahill found out he was going to be getting his daughter he felt like a figure skater getting a gold figure. It was time for Cabella, Amory, and him to retreat to another country. Cahill couldn't risk anything or anyone from his past or Amory's mother finding them, harming them, or dividing them so he told Cabella to get their passports ready and as soon as Cahill's plane landed back in Michigan he was going to take Amory straight to his people to get a quick, fake passport. The United States wasn't shit, but a burden on their backs and it was time for each of them to get a clean slate.

Speed-walking through the St. Louis- Lambert International Airport, this was about to be the fastest plane Cahill ever boarded. He had Charlotte's money already transferred on a money card so that end of the bargain was covered so all he had to do was arrive now. All Cahill could think about was seeing his daughter for the first time. What she will look like and if she would look more like her mother Omani or him. How she would adapt to him? If the first time he held her she was going to cry uncontrollably or was she going to be nothing more than a happy baby picking up on her father's scent, touch, voice, and presence.

"My plane has landed where are we meeting?"

"I'm glad you had a safe flight now meet me at the water tower on 2nd Street South. It's a giant ass landmark you can't miss it."

Charlotte was sad to say goodbye to Amory since she had grown so attached to her, but technically Amory was her little cousin so she would always be able to keep tabs on her. Amory deserved to be raised by people that loved her; whatever issues was going on between Cahill and Amory's mother was between them. All Charlotte wanted to do was secure Amory and secure herself.

Once at the landmark Cahill damn near cried.

"Amory, hi Amory," Cahill grabbed his daughter from Charlotte and held her close to him.

"She is so beautiful Charlotte she looks like a blend of me and her mother. Thank you for getting her to me safely."

"Yeah whatever, I'm really going to miss the kid so I think y'all should just go before I start getting all mushy."

"Okay, I don't want this part to be hard so here's a card and it has 75,000 on it more money then we discussed. I feel like you deserve it because Lindsay could've killed you, your my blood, and I'm the one that got you tangled up in this jumble with me. I didn't know it would lead to me gaining my daughter, but for that I am thankful and I hope you spend that money wisely and stay out of trouble. Virginia is a beautiful city maybe you should start over here while you here."

"I was thinking the same thing Cahill. I hope you and Amory have a nice life. I was just trying to do the right thing."

"Say bye cousin Charlotte," Cahill told Amory already high in daddy mode and Amory just smiled at Charlotte as always. The exchange was easy; it seemed like Amory was going to do exceptional with her father, Charlotte had a pocket full of money to keep her out of harm's way, and now Amory and Cahill had to board a plane so they could make it home.

Chapter 17: Cycle Concealer

Being criminal minded wasn't exactly Gab's prowess, but being vengeful was. The philosophy of being a part of a motorcycle horde entailed a couple key points. All Gab had to do was state his internal affairs and his gang would do his dirty work.

The Monarchs were sticking it to the Mitchell's and affiliates of the Mitchell's. Boredom was starting to pollute the atmosphere so now it was time to crank up the violence again. What was left to do to Omani and Onyx besides murdering them? The Monarchs didn't have time to be on some Hannibal or cannibal shit so one clicks homicides would be the aftermath of their detainment.

"I'm goin give y'all four minutes to say y'all goodbyes to each other. I would've thought that Smoke would've been to the rescue by now, but since he's a no show we can just wipe y'all off the map and keep it pushing," Gab clarified.

"You sure are mighty laid-back with killing your own fam like you did this before so what other family members of ours have you killed?"

"That's nonya Omani."

"Why kill us when y'all can just leave us out here in the middle of nowhere stranded?"

"No can do little sister; never leave any witnesses behind who are liable to rat you out to the feds."

"Your dumbass then kidnapped the wrong sister. You should've kidnapped our sister Kyra. Smoke hates me and I hate him and I hate his bitch ass wife Passive so I highly doubt he will come for me I been switched teams baby. Why don't you let me kill both Smoke and Passive because clearly you or your timid ass squad doesn't have the gulls to do it. I've been doing shady shit to everybody in my family since day one. Your punk ass is just getting started."

"So you got street cred then? More street cred then what the street critics are aware of huh?"

"Sure do back to back."

"So prove yourself to me by killing your baby daddy right now." Gab freed Omani of her bondages and handed her his gun as his crew stood around her with a circle of firearms scattered amongst her in case she pulled the trigger on the wrong victim. Omani just stood up still in the nude like she was posing for an artist using her arms and her hands to cover up some of her body parts.

Onyx just sat there like an iron curtain. He hoped there was a method to Omani's madness and she wasn't going to kill her baby daddy to save herself for real. They didn't come this far for Omani to just become a one man team. Omani was as serious as a drill sergeant instructing his cadets.

"No problem; this ain't my baby daddy so his death means nothing to me. I'm sorry Onyx for misleading you, but that's what I do. I'm shady down to the plasma in my bones and you know that granted you still loved me unconditionally. I didn't think we were going to get serious again so I met a man who happens to be a mayor and I started fucking him. Long behold, Mayor Cahill is my baby's father not you. "

"Stop shitting on me Omani don't turn shady on me." Confusion was the conclusion to sum up Onyx's current mental state. There was no way the woman he just left his hometown with breaking laws with would just betray him so easily; especially not after he tried to protect her from being gang-banged and videotaped. Those images of her being fucked by a bottle throttle will live with him forever, but still he didn't view Omani any differently than before.

"I'm not so please don't take this personal baby."

"Wait, since we being honorary let me tell you something. Let me give you a real reason to kill me," Onyx interjected.

"What is it?" Omani asked with the gun raised high.

"I have another child with another woman somewhere out there in the world."

Instantly, Omani pulled the trigger to the brain like a gun veteran. Blood splattered everywhere like a Michael Myers scene; the Monarchs were in disbelief. Omani was clearly the total opposite of Smoke; cop and stone cold killer. Now the Monarchs were beginning to question who the hell they kidnapped. Maybe they would've been better off killing Omani and not Onyx or both, but instead Gab wanted to entertain Omani and her antics.

"Your Tomb Raider ass just shot your baby daddy."

"I just told you and everybody else out here he is not the daddy. Now you see I'm about my business so what up? Am I still your hostage or are we going to take them out? You tryna play this fish and bait shit when you need to run this war. The fuck y'all acting like some pussycats for; this is only two people we are talking about. Y'all must not want to kill them; just torture them a bit and keep it pushing?"

"Two people who are pros at dodging death. How else can you kill them without luring them? Don't fucking question how or when I take care of my beef shawty. You really expect me to believe you actually are willing to kill your brother and sister-in-law?"

"I am straight up."

"Why you wanna kill them so bad? You know once their gone their gone."

"They are the reason why my daughter, my 1st child was kidnapped from me so that shit is unforgivable. I will kill anybody over my daughter and if I don't hurry up and get her back, her father might try to get her. I can't have that I'll never see her again."

"You say you got street cred; how do I know you ain't goin use your cred to kill me or my crew or anybody in my crew?"

"Y'all can let me go and get back to my journey or I can ride out with y'all and do this thang the way y'all should've done this thing instead of riding y'all asses to Missouri to hunt me down. The decision is up to you and your crew; if you can't make your own decisions and you need a little outside help I'm here."

Omani was real sharp and blunt with her words even to someone who held her life in the palm of their hands.

"Look you little shady insignificant black sheep you need to fly right because the more you talk the more I want to kill you. You out your rabbit ass mind if you think I'm goin just set you free just because you killed somebody. What you did do was earn some respect and some clothes, but I don't have you in my custody for nothing. Your ass ain't leaving here until your brother comes to get you so if

he never comes to get you, your ass will never leave."

Chapter 18: White Lava

Back in the flash where women misuse and abuse friendship was a very intriguing memory. Both Lindsay and Omani were candidly invited to a classic all-white yacht party. Whoever the rich party-thrower was bared gifts too. Their invitation included complements from Kate Spade accessories, dresses distinctively designed by Vera Wang, and matching heels by Gianvito Rossi. All Cahill had to do was call a secretary and all the sizes he needed was given.

Omani's hot, fertile ass had never even been on a yacht, to a yacht party, or received extravagant gifts from someone just because of association. Omani naively thought that Lindsay was a loyal friend and felt lucky to be receiving the fruits of their friendship. Typical female friendships consisted of regular, low-class, city dangling shit. If Omani wasn't so blinded by opulence she would've been able to foresee Lindsay's true intentions.

Ready to show up and show out with her ace boon coon, Omani couldn't wait to board the yacht with Lindsay and then she called.

"What up doll?"

"I just want to let you know I can't attend the yacht party with you tonight. I got too much business to tend too in my office. I need you to represent for the both of us."

"Business huh? Why can't Nestle handle it? Isn't that what you have an assistant for anyway?"

"And an assistant assists and in order for her to be assisted somebody has to be there to give her orders. Stop acting like this is going to be the last yacht party in the universe. It's just a silly old party; I been to plenty of those. You got some nice gifts out the deal and trust me you want miss me so just chill and have fun and you better call me tomorrow and tell me all the gossip."

"Sure I'll make sure I do that," Omani lied. Omani didn't like the fact that she was about to go hang out with somebody else's friends without being properly introduced. Omani didn't have a problem flying solo, hell now without Lindsay being there she could really turn up. She was going to put on her fly ass gifts and run the night. When Omani reached the dock to board the mega boat that sat before her eyes she was so intrigued.

"I've never seen any woman look as spectacular as you do in anything I've ever brought a woman," a man disconnected her sight-seeing.

"You must buy women gifts all the time then. You better watch it those women are going to start using you for your gifts"

"I don't and trust me a woman will never be able to use me; I only buy gifts in celebration of something."

"What are we celebrating tonight then?"

"We're going to celebrate this being a wonderful night and our first encounter."

"So I take it this is your boat and your party?"

"Yeah it is. Where's Lindsay she usually never misses any party I throw especially when I coerce her with gifts."

"She's stuck in the office doing work."

"I'm happy she sent you to come out and play with me."

"I don't play games with men. I don't know what you and Lindsay do together, but that has nothing to do with me. If she sucked your dick or fondled your balls to get these gifts you can have them back right now and I'll leave this party naked."

"Me and Lindsay have and will never cross the lines of business, but me and you on the other hand, if you want to get naked you can just come to my room and let me suck on your tits and titillate your clit."

"That's all you goin do?"

"No, I have way more in store for you."

Leading Omani into his humongous yacht master bedroom, Cahill was sizing her rosebud up as she peered into his white heaven. All he had to do was untie the bowtie around her neck which he did sparingly and she was innocently bare. Cahill didn't waste any time planting kisses all over her body prepping for his entrance. Off rip, Cahill knew he had that tap out dick, but he was going to make Omani handle every inch of him without fear.

Upon entrance, Omani shivered and quivered and tried to put a force field up against Cahill, but he was too abrasive to stop. Fighting the pain side of pleasure, Cahill yanked Omani by her hair and gave her a pep talk.

"If you want this dick you better take it; relax ma and internalize that pain as pleasure." After a few inhales and exhales, Omani begin to open up without tensing up letting Cahill sink deeper and deeper into her riverfront. That night, Omani and Cahill fucked on every rail, open space, and room they could on the yacht making Omani experience four different types of orgasms she probably never knew existed. Triggering a sexual mania, Cahill and Omani were overzealously aroused with one another; they fucked so much that Omani got pregnant. Omani couldn't help herself, Cahill's kielbasa was better than her other nigga or any nigga that ever penetrated her twat. Pregnancy made Omani snap out her sexual trance

Lindsay purposely didn't attend the yacht party with Cahill. She wanted Omani and Cahill to meet because he was a good-looking thundercat and Omani was a young, sultry tenderoni Cahill would melt over. Why not set-up your ex-lover's sister with his enemy? You never know what could happen when two human beings bound to be attracted to each other will try to kindle. Not at all did Lindsay think her plan would backfire in her face and even if it did it was worth it.

Chapter 19: A Brother's Fury

The 11th precinct hadn't had any contact from their

captain Smoke in weeks and didn't know anything about

the complications that had been emerging into his life. All

they knew was that he was taking some time off for some

family matters. Black received the call on the anonymous

tip line for a UPS package shipping from Missouri was

supposed to contain some hardcore evidence. Once the

UPS package arrived, Black called an emergency meeting

with all the officers so they could preview this crime-

solving evidence together. Black popped the tape in the

DVD drive while all the officers had their eyes wide and

their pens ready to stride on the lines of their yellow pads.

Starting off the tape was distant photos of a bunch of

motorists and their motorcycles. Following those sneak

previews was Cruise's vile message to Smoke and then

came the boom; a naked body; a smoking hot naked body.

The officers saw Smoke's sister Omani bonded to a

motorcycle, get cold duck poured on her, then watched her get fucked by a bottle in her ass and vagina. Black rushed to push stop on the derogatory DVD they were fooled by.

"That's my little cousin man; she just had a baby. Who does this type of shit?" Smoke's cousin Rellow complained exiting the room in disgust.

"This was supposed to be police evidence and this is evidence for Smoke so who's gonna tell him about this?" Black questioned, but none of the officers answered they all just begin to gloat their eyeballs off into space. Everybody knew that Smoke would go to war for his sister and he was going to be fuming when he found out about this. Nobody wanted to heighten Smoke's temper because he was hot-headed without a temper.

"So y'all goin make me tell him huh?" Black analyzed.

$

When Passive, Smoke, and Corbin reached Lafayette, Indiana it was time for them to touch down. Smoke and Passive were now going to be residing in a 1400 square foot fully furnished downtown apartment there. Their apartment had a skylight, an open concept architecture design, a soaking tub, a great central location plus more. Everything about the apartment screamed perfect serenity for Passive who just wanted to enjoy the rest of her pregnancy.

Passive hadn't seen a doctor since she fled the hospital. Since she needed daily monitoring and care. She found herself a house doctor by the name of Dr, Moore and she was supposed to be making her first visit today.

"Smoke, your phone is ringing," Passive disrupted Smoke who was too caught up in rubbing Passive's belly and listening to the baby's heartbeat to hear his phone.

"Okay, I'll be right back babies," Smoke claimed speaking of Passive and the baby she was carrying.

It was Officer Black, "what's up Black? How's everything at the department been running?"

"The department should be the least of your concern Smoke. I called you to talk to you about your sister Omani."

"She was just kidnapped; I thought that would've slowed her hot ass down for a minute. What could she have possibly done now?"

"Some motorcycle crew made a tape of them sexually accosting her butt-naked on top of a bike with a champagne bottle in her ass and in her woo-ha. That pack of scumbags sent the tape to the office as spam for evidence. Ain't no telling what else they going to do to her man; they on some barbarous shit."

"Fuck!" Smoke tried to yell lightly so he wouldn't alarm Passive.

"What are you going to do Smoke?"

"I don't know Omani is the one who got herself in this shit and I cannot leave Passive's side right now. You better guard that tape with your life and make sure nobody I mean nobody better not be able to press they eyes or they hands on that tape."

"I got you Smoke, I'll secure it somewhere."

It took everything in Smoke's power for him not to punch a hole in the wall, but he couldn't do that him and Passive just got their apartment and they were renting it. Ain't nobody have time to be coming out they pocket for damage fees or forfeiting their security deposit.

This shit was becoming too surreal especially as it relates to Gab who was his own flesh and blood. *"How could you kidnap your own cousin and then let your boys film her and lay hands and objects in/on her in such a degrading fashion? Then to top it off you goin send the fucking tape to my job so all the niggas in my job can be all up in my business having wet dreams about my baby sister."*

Something had to give, but whatever it was, Smoke had to stick by Passive's side because Omani made her bed; now she had to lie in it. Nobody told her to take her dumbass up to Missouri trying to disturb people's lives or kill whoever she killed in the boonies. It was time for her to learn a lesson of loyalty the hard way.

$

While, British and Sina were on their way to Kentucky, Rue finally decided to shoot British a text or two. He shot her a couple of screenshots of gaudy, glimmering engagement rings asking her which one did she like best A, B, C, or D.

"He's got to be playing tricks on me; I know he's playing tricks on me."

"What are you ranting about British?"

"I think my boyfriend is going to propose to me; we got to postpone this trip. I need you turn this thing around and drive us to Michigan. We can get back on the road after

I get my ring, but before I catch up with my bae I need you to stop in Marquette. My cousin is pregnant and I need to check on her; I'm the only person who is going to do that. Plus I can share with her face to face about what we did to Miss Kyra. She's going to get a kick out of that, but at least you'll see where I get my craziness from."

"I'm so ecstatic I can't wait to meet her," Sina pretended to be enthused even though she wasn't looking forward to seeing anymore new faces especially nobody who had similar traits to British.

"

Chapter 20: The Big Showdown

On Lindsay's heels like a pair of socks, Elvia and

Posh felt closer and closer to finding her. At address

number two Paradise begged for a piece of the action.

"Y'all know I'm not the enemy anymore so y'all

can include me in."

"Bitch please say something else stupid and we goin

duct tape your mouth and see how you like breathing then."

"Okay, damn y'all ain't got to be so mean."

"I'm sure Lindsay would love to see you betrayed

her to work with us."

"What you mean Lindsay? Is that who y'all looking

for? If so, I'm good handcuff me, duct tape my mouth. I'll

zip my on lips shut. "

"You still think that bitch trying to kill you huh?"

Both Elvia and Posh laughed at Paradise's fright. They left

her to go snuff out any living people in address number

two. As Elvia and Posh were crossing the street to

address#2 Lindsay was coming down the street and seen two strange women snooping around her old house and a car parked in front of her property.

"What the fuck are they doing?" Lindsay asked herself.

"I haven't had a lessee for that house in months and why the fuck is they vehicle parked on my property. If they have business across the street then they need to move they piece of shit across the street with them.

Driving past the abandoned vehicle, Lindsay saw a woman inside the vehicle so she figured she would get out of her car and politely ask the woman to move the car off of her property. Lindsay pulled slightly in her driveway than got out to approach the woman sitting in the car.

"Excuse me, excuse me," Lindsay banged on the window.

Paradise wanted to conceal her handcuffs, but how could she; she was cuffed to the passenger grab handler in the backseat. Maybe she could camouflage them somehow, but how could she do that with her posture being so obvious and no free hands.

Paradise used her elbow to roll the window down a bit so she can talk.

"Yes ma'am how you doing?"

"I'll be doing fine when you move this aluminum crap off my property. Are those two girls who crossed the street your friends?" Listening to the voice precisely, Paradise realized the bitch she was talking too was Lindsay. She was ready to panic, but she had to keep her cool. She didn't want to scare Lindsay away. Not to mention a quick look at Lindsay and Paradise noticed she was pregnant by her round-shaped belly.

"Yes, those are my friends; they saw that house on the market and wanted to check it out for themselves."

"I own that house so let them know if they are interested, they can just ring my gate, and I'll buzz them in.

I'll cut them a deal today; I thought they were just some trespassers." Lindsay had never seen Paradise a day in her life so it didn't dawn on her that the flea bag who didn't kill Passive months ago was right before her very eyes.

"I'm sure it's a billion people who live in that pretty ass house so who should they ask for?"

"They should ask for Mrs. Chambers or call me Lindsay." Lindsay noticed a gleaming necklace around Paradise's neck that said her name. Since it wasn't too many bitches on planet Earth whose mother named them Paradise, Lindsay assumed something fishy was going on. Jumping into protection mode, Lindsay grabbed a rock to break the car's back window. She began taking the rock and pounding Paradise with it.

"I told you to kill Passive, but you didn't then you show up at my house to do what?" Lindsay pounded and pounded Paradise like she was a bag of ice.

"Help mc! Help! Please! Help me!"

"Oh, now you want to call for help now that I'm taking this rock and breaking you with it." Immediately, Elvia and Posh ran to Paradise's aid after hearing her cries for help and something shatter. Upon reaching the car, Posh and Elvia noticed a woman beating Paradise lifeless with a big object so they started shooting at the woman. Car window glass was breaking everywhere.

"It's her, it's her, its Lindsay!" Paradise screamed barely able to speak because that rock thrashing was silencing her, but that only made Lindsay hit Paradise harder and stronger and yank the car door open so she could drag Paradise out of the car and continue beating her ass all the way to her driveway. Something was stopping Lindsay from grabbing Paradise.

"What type of fucking friends leaves you handcuffed to a car handler?" Seething with anger, Lindsay split the handcuffs in half. Bullets kept flying her way and she kept dodging them using Paradise as a shield and a punching bag, but then a stray bullet hit Paradise now she was dead and gone.

"Don't fuck up my car we got to ride in that. Let's shoot her tires out so she can't go anywhere and spray her car with bullets. Running to her car, Lindsay tried not to stick herself on any glass. Now that her car was just assassinated by bullets she needed an escape plan.

Burning rubber down the street a strange car whipped up in her driveway behind her vehicle. British saw glass everywhere, a body on the pavement, and Lindsay stooped down on the side of her car. Lindsay trusted her instincts, leaped into the vehicle, and let them take off.

"What the fuck is going on Lindsay?"

"I don't know them bitches finally found me."

"Wait, who the fuck is this? Why is she riding you around like you a millionaire or something?"

"This is my new friend Sina and we just saved your black ass so don't question us. What bitches are you speaking of?"

"Some of Smoke and Passive bitches' I guess and now they got Paradise. Dirty motherfuckers! I don't know why they haven't sliced her throat. Maybe they were bringing her to me so I could I don't know."

"Is the baby okay?"

"The baby is fine just get me out of here and keep me out of here."

Aggravated, Elvia and Posh got in her wrecked car ready to stop at the nearest dealership and cash out on a brand new whip.

"We almost had her Elvia now we got to disappoint three people."

"I know Posh, we can't beat ourselves up to bad. At least we tried."

Chapter 21: Exit # Shady

What a paradox; Tia couldn't stand trial. The judge ruled her to be mentally incompetent and shipped her ass to a popular institute where all the crazies go in Michigan. Same place Lindsay Chambers and Liz Chambers were housed at which was the Rose Hill Center. I don't what made authorities think that this place was going to resolve anything for Tia. If anything it was just going to make her condition worst. Just look at how Lindsay turnt out, she went from crazy to mentally insane.

Before the mental cops took Tia away she begged her judge to lock her ass up in prison.

"Judge Judy please reconsider! I rather take a sentence! I rather go to prison! Send me to prison! I didn't do these heinous crimes I'm being accused of!"

The judge just slammed her mallet on her pallet.

"Order in the court; the sentence has been made. Get her out of here!"

On the way to the nut house Tia was in a big stupor. Who in the hell was goin come visit her in a crazy house? Guess there goes her best friend, any friend, any associate, or anybody that once had respect for her. Who was goin come visit her anyway after they found out that she murdered her own son who didn't even make it to his 1st birthday? She wondered was Rue going to kill her like he swore he was if the law didn't give her a suitable punishment. Let's not forget about British; she wondered if British was going to come share the DNA results with her and then ridicule her for being a total fuck-up. Not only did Tia fuck-up relationships, but she fucked up homes and families; her own blended family to be exact. This was about to be hell for Tia who was about to be drugged up every hour, sitting in a white room with the walls closing in on her, and staring out a high-rise window like a senior citizen in a nursing home., but this was the destiny she chose.

$

Eagerly, waiting on Smoke to return back to Michigan, Rock knew Smoke was trying to protect Passive so he prepared himself for a solo mission. It wasn't going to be no more waiting on Smoke because Smoke had more important priorities. Besides, Rock was a security powerhouse so his intelligence was enough to take down Cahill in close-range or even 10 miles away.

Rock was very emotional when he heard the news about Paradise, but what could he do? If death was her fate then it was her fate. It wasn't her future with Rock that killed her; it was her past with Lindsay that put her in the crossfire. Soon as Rock was healed from that hernia, Cahill was going to be deader than a squirrel on roadside.

$

Settled in Uruguay, South America Cahill was content with the choice that he made for his blended family. Uruguay is the least corrupt country in Latin

America, never experienced a recession when recessions where concurrent around the planet, housing costs were lower, food costs were lower, and health care costs were lower. There were an abundance of benefits in Uruguay's economy, atmosphere, and environment than any state in the U.S. could've offered them. Amory was adjusting well to Cahill being her father and Cabella being her real stepmother. Not to mention Cahill changed Amory's name to Amory Caesar; he had to so she could carry on her father's legacy. Being around Amory was beginning to make Cabella want to have some kids of her own and of course the big M for marriage. Traditional in values, it had to be marriage first then kids. Both Cahill and Cabella found work in Uruguay fast except Cabella found herself a new passion that was beginning to rub Cahill the wrong way.

It was so many clothing, shoes, and purse designers in Uruguay who all wanted a beautifully, sculptured woman like Cabella to be their ambassador model. As always, Cahill's insecurities started kicking in and Cahill didn't want Cabella modeling. He didn't want every man in Uruguay looking at his woman's body in a sex-appealing way, which was contradictory because it was fine when Cabella was showing off her cleavage and wearing short skirts giving weather forecasts on the local news. As hard it was, Cahill was trying his best not to resort back to the old Cahill and be the good guy for once against all odds and evens.

$

Unbeknownst was Lindsay's mother house being her new haven since Passive and Elvia had already been there and done that. That house was still a luxurious continental house and it belonged to British so why not stay with her new accomplice. Even though, she didn't want to be shacking up with a young couple, British was good company and so was Sina their new family friend. Rue did end up proposing to British and she accepted his proposal with confidence. She had a rock bigger than any diamond on a New York red carpet so wedding arrangements was in progress.

Both Sina and British shared with Lindsay about how they left Kyra in the lake and that tickled Lindsay she thought that shit was brilliant. Not in a billion years would Lindsay have thought of that.

Elmira, the babysitter of Nestle's daughter Natalie reported Nestle missing to the police after she never returned to pick up her daughter. Police had been waiting for somebody to come forward about Nestle Parks because Nestle was more than missing she was dead and investigations were pending for a murder/homicide. The police had seized Nestle's Audi from Downtown which still had all of her belongings in it which was evidence A and then from the fire in Hines Park they found skeletal remains and now they were finally able to use DNA samples to make a match for.

Elmira was willing to adapt Natalie so the Chamber's didn't have to worry about that and the only person Elmira knew to contact in relationship to Nestle was Lindsay because that was her boss. Once Elmira shared Lindsay with the awful news of the loss of Nestle, in Lindsay's head she just convicted Passive of everything.

"I know Passive did this, but it's cool I got something for that ass."

$

Its ill-fated Elvia and Posh didn't achieve in killing Lindsay; they figured they would distance themselves from Passive and Smoke for awhile. They didn't want to stick around to see the effects or disaffects of Lindsay's pregnancy and very subsistence against Smoke's and Passive's marriage. They decided they would do Smoke a favor and go after his rebellious ass baby sister since it was partially Elvia's fault why Omani was kidnapped in the first place. As Elvia recalls, she tried to stop Passive from belittling The Monarchs, but like always Passive insisted on doing things her way. Nevertheless, Elvia and the crew knew what Omani did in Michigan before she ended in Missouri and her recent feelings about her brother and sister-in-law. The only thing the crew didn't know was who was all involved in the killing, who exactly was killed, and why. Truth was, they was better off going on a vacation somewhere like Costa Rico then going to salvage such a rotten ass apple like Omani.

$

Like always Passive and Smoke were undividable, but since Elvia and Posh didn't succeed in killing Lindsay Smoke had to be the bearer of bad news.

"Passive, I have to tell you something critical please don't be mad at me. Please, please don't be mad at me."

"Oh my God; I don't even want to know. What did you do now Darnell?"

"It's about Lindsay," Passive had an incoming call.

"Hold that thought Smoke I'm going to go answer that," Passive planted two fingers over Smoke's lips.

"Hello."

"Diamond, what's good with you, I mean Passive." Passive knew that screechy voice from anywhere."

"What do you want now Lindsay?"

"I see you sent two of your best trained dikes to kill me and I see y'all kidnapping my rivals. What are we on the same team now? Are you finally seeing beyond those red, white, and blue police lights?"

"I don't know what the fuck your talking about Lindsay. I didn't send anybody to kill you. It's not enough time in the day for me to waste it thinking about you."

"That was harsh, but what's even harsher is that you killed my assistant Nestle and broke into my office and pocketed some of my files. Is your clip empty yet?"

"I've been out of the game and in the hospital pregnant so you got the wrong enemy." Lindsay almost dropped her phone out of her hand.

"Did you just say your pregnant?"

"Yeah that's right I'm pregnant as hell now let me tell you what I know. I know you've been working with Cahill, that's my godfather bitch. Who the fuck side did you think he was really going to be on? Yours? Telling him he got 90 days to kill me bitch you got one bite to eat some poison and die," Passive lied knowing she got her ammo from Rock.

"I can't die because I'm pregnant too. Since you know every got damn thing did your hubby tell you that or he hasn't had the gall to run that by you yet?"

"I hope that baby dies in your stomach because you impregnated yourself. You stole my husband's sperm."

Lindsay laughed uproariously. "Ha, ha, ha that's what you think? He gladly came in me every time I let him loose to have sex with me," Lindsay fibbed.

"Bitch bye; get the fuck off of my line." Passive ended Lindsay's ignorance to transfer her anger to Smoke."

"Get your ass in here now Darnell!" Smoke knew he had done something wrong; he should've been eavesdropping on his wife instead of giving her privacy.

"Yes Passive?"

"So when in the fuck were you going to tell me that your ex-crackbrained bitch was pregnant with your baby?"

"I was never going to tell you that Passive; I sent Elvia and Posh to kill her and the baby, but they failed."

"You fucking failed me! How in the fuck could you fail me Darnell? I trusted you!" Passive stared at Smoke with a polka facc.

"You can stay in this apartment by yourself; Fuck all this shit! I don't want it anymore; I don't want you anymore. I want a new fucking identity. I'm so fucking sick of you, Omani, and fucking Lindsay! I've never had to deal with such oblivion in my life!"

"Passive I know this is upsetting, but please don't leave and calm down. At least wait until after you have the baby. You know you can't be getting upset right now. This is a stress-free zone remember?"

While Passive was making big, bad decisions she was throwing on her shoes, threw on a sweater, grabbed her purse, and grabbed her car keys. "I can't be around you any longer even your vibe is venomous so take your fucking ring and leave me and the baby alone!" Passive removed her ring from her ring finger and threw it at Smoke like it was a penny. Why was Passive so mad when she just defended Smoke? She was done being a wife, a hostage, a killer, and a drug-transporter; she just wanted to be a mother now.

Exiting the house, Passive got in her car and turned on the ignition. Before she could even push the gas pedal down she felt a big gush in between her legs. Her amniotic sac just ruptured and now she was delirious and outside in a fucking car. No matter what though she was not going back in that god-forsaken house with that low down dirty shame of a man she called a husband. She backed out the driveway and was just going to hash and rehash out things as she periled down the broken, solid yellow and white traffic lines illustrated on the roadway ahead.

TO BE CONTINUED...

"

Thank you for tuning into the Shady Series! A shady spinoff could be under construction; you'll just have to keep tuning into the works of Cheraee C. to find out and see.

Please take the time out to leave Cheraee C. a book review on Amazon.com or Mocypublishing.com regarding any or all of her novels after reading them including:

Another Shady Mission

Liq-Trocity

On Another Shady Mission

The Shadiest Mission Ever

If you're interested in book publishing Mocy Publishing is accepting submissions please visit:

www.mocypublishing.com